THE RUBICON

poems and short fiction

Also by J.B. Hogan

Losing Cotton
Living Behind Time
Angels In The Ozarks
The Apostate

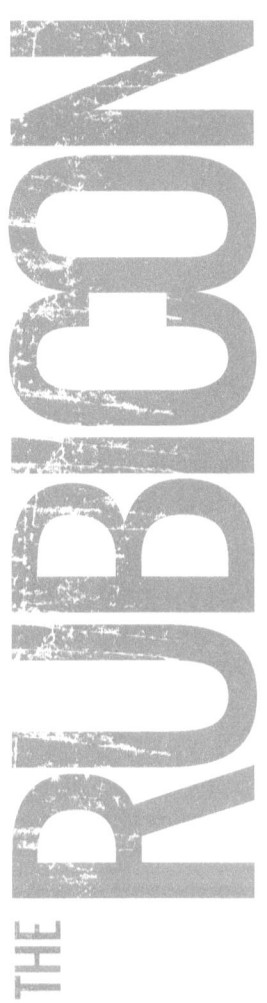

THE RUBICON

J.B. HOGAN

TWEED PRESS

AN IMPRINT OF

OGHMA CREATIVE MEDIA

Tweed Press
Oghma Creative Media
Fayetteville, AR 72703

www.oghmacreative.com

The characters and events in this book are fictitious.
Any similarity to real persons, living or dead, is entirely
coincidental and not intended by the author.

ISBN: 978-1-63373-109-7

Interior Design and Editing by Casey W. Cowan

acknowledgements

With appreciation to the following journals in which the poems and stories of this collection first appeared, at times in different versions and with different titles:

Poetry Credits:

Poesia: "You're Always There," "Your Poem (As If)," "Aqui no se Rinde Nadie," "Rice Paddies Lost," "God Is a Metaphor," "Blue Haze at Milepost 279," "Merida," "Political Sigh," "The Rubicon," "Just Half Done," "Half-Century Beats," and "Jacky Kerwacky Riding the 242"

Mastodon Dentist: "Reminder"

Poets Against War: "Some Places We've Been"

The Swallow's Tail: "Cadaver," "Something Lost—A Night of Stars," and "Full Faded"

Every Day Poets: "There Are Buffalo," "Braceros," "It's Not

About Me," "Hemingway Hotel," "End Game," "The Plague," "George Bernard Shaw," "Isiolo," "Nairobi," and "Ice Storm"

Aphelion: "Metamorphosis," "Alien," "It Is," "Chameleon Boy," "Reservation," "Decade," "Nothing Up Ahead," "Holy Leper," "Your Dewy Throne," and "A Form of Ashes"

Cynic Online Magazine: "Gray Man," and "Cadillac Mountain"

The Ranfurly Review: "The Wind" and "Corridors"

Word Catalyst: "Ameca Ameca," "Borinquen Exile," "Gentle Day with Light Breeze," "Yellow Aspen Leaves," "Pre-Dawn Gray," "Forgotten Pages," "Wind Turbines-Eastern New Mexico," "Blind Kid's Cry," and "Big Houses"

Guerrilla Pamphlets: "Borinquen Exile" (reprint), "If Anything Were Wrong," "Gabriel Heatter Mornings," "Six Blocks from the Zocalo," "Hotel Papagayo-Cuernavaca, Mexico," "Good Friday-Leon, Nicaragua," "I Thought I Heard," "Locked Turnstile and Barbed Wire," and "El Coral"

ken*again: "Wind Turbines—Eastern New Mexico" (reprint), "In His Presence," "A Little History"

Dead Mule: "Thomas Wolfe Saw James Joyce," "The Old Man," "The Pyramid Outside Puebla," "Empire Reborn," "Eroding Lions," "Your Little Rabbi," "How White," "Gorki in New York," "Dissolving to Nothing," "He Was a Big Man," "He Was Fallen," "Through the Years," "Looking Back," "Red Brick House," "New Year's Eve—Mazatlan," "Orphan," and "To Stop a Cockfight"

Bewildering Stories: "Flashback" and "Mushroom Visions"

Kalkion: "Rainmaker," "Middle Ground," "First Things First," "It's Hard to Imagine You as a Woman," "Feeling Gray," "Open Casket," "Time Became an Arrow," "Listen Up, America," "Playa del Carmen," "I Wasn't There When He Died," "Dad," "Inoperative," "Man of Straw," "Pack Runner," and "Grocery List"

Underground Voices: "I Get That a Lot," "When You Died" and "Bullet"

Copperfield Review: "The Villa at Gaspra," "Through the Pass," "Faulkner in Paris," "Reading a Dickens Biography in Spanish—Puerto Escondido, Mexico," "Dickens in America," "Semenovski Square," "Xochicalco," "Anecdote of the Jaw: Wallace Stevens and a Large Puddle of Water," "A Dry Country," "Circling a Famous Author," and "Avenue of the Dead—Teotihuacan"

Blue Lake Review: "Sandinista Homes"

vox poetica: "Storm Over North Africa" and "Reading Don Quixote—San Miguel de Allende"

Poems also included in anthologies: "It's Not About Me" and "End Game" in Every Day Poets, Two; "George Bernard Shaw" in Every Day Poets, Three (forthcoming)

Story Credits:

Dead Mule: "December, 1967"

Rumble: "Mercado"

Ranfurly Review: "He Was Lying in a Hammock"

Crack the Spine: "An Awesome Poet"

Gloom Cupboard: "Hemingway Hotel" and "Hitchin' Out"

Medulla Review: "Janey"

Word Catalyst: "The Old Man" and "Kerosene Heat"

Raving Dove: "$150 Per"

Kalkion: "An Old Dream," "La Mordida," "Sea Plane," and "Just His Luck"

Smokebox: "Once in a Lifetime," "On the Golf Course," "Southern Hospitality," A Small Concussion" and "A Loud Hum"

Avatar Review: "Down from the Country Club"

The Square Table: "Hurricane"

Megaera: "He Liked It That Much"

contents

You're Always There

You're always there,
somewhere—coming up from behind;
a shadow on a moonless night,
an empty line on a blank page,
a dream where you don't belong.

You're always there,
always will be,
insisting it's possible to
catch your shadow
write your memory
dream your absence.

You're always there,
maddeningly pure, ethereal,
waiting for the inevitable surrender,
these many years hence,
to the magnificent obscenity
of your boundless, passionate need.

Reminder

Before sky light blue,
finger-thin pines weave and flow
wind's soft whistle through branches noisesome
like a reminder softly spoken
of coming time's cessation.

Tomorrow—if it should be—beckons little
these days of late fall warmth and
leaves down-drifting, landing
landing on the brown wet turf
collecting in a thick compost lair.

Today—all that is—is little
this moment of time outshooting, missing
missing the target always
drifting like a bolt bad-hurled.

Yesterday—it has been—shows little
those years of backward gold
memory refailing, lighting
lighting on the shiny sod
forgotten like a thought well old.

Behind gray needles skyward,
washed blue backwash on canvas unfolds
wind's fingertip touch on bark and limb echoing
like a reminder quietly whispered
of ebbing life's completion.

*Aquí no se rinde nadie**

Pale moon above Managua
soft light on empty, silent streets
van rumbling through tin roofed barrios
    of scrap wood and dirt
night of incessant roosters, smoke burning fields
fenceless, dusty ballparks, littered and bare
overstuffed buses, broken down trucks—
but tomorrow there's Jesus in the streets, Calvary replayed
and a growing black market, dead soldiers at the front.

Many sided Nicaragua, enigma and hope
which of you is real, who guides your path?
Is Daniel really there?
Or does it go of its own, its disciplined will?
Barricaded against enemy
behind walls of pride, of fear.
What sustains you Nicaragua—
    an aging dream?
    the energy of memory?

New Nicaragua—so difficult, desperate
    —alone
shoulders into the wind, the land, the war
bone marrow certain of your unrepeatable past.
Unchanging Nicaragua, stubborn and bold
    conqueror's prize.
Yet unrelenting Nicaragua, too,
as sure of waiting pain
     sacrifice
     death
as in resolve that no intruder shall pass
into the land—ever again.

Nobody here gives up.

Rice Paddies Lost

From the bank above we watched it,
my brother and I,
watched it pass below,
like a loud metal river
winding along a curving steel course.
The tracks rising, lifting, rising, lifting,
counting out the sound
in the cool morning air.

Flat cars stretched back
far beyond the bend
as far as you could see;
a slender ribbon of gray and green—
and on the flat cars
trucks, jeeps, and
tanks.

And on the tanks, jeeps,
and trucks
were men, khaki-uniformed heroes,
down there waving,
smiling at us.

Smiling up at us on the bank,
we who could scarcely imagine,
we who could little know,
that the red blood of heroes,
even that of men such as these,
could be surprised
from its cathedral of flesh and
trickle down rocky, distant hills
to mingle with the murky water of
rice paddies lost and unremembered.

Long, Forgotten Tracks

"Frank," Pete Mason called from the back yard, "come here. Look!"

Frank, at the kitchen sink helping his mother dry dishes, tossed his towel down and raced through the house, past the stairs to the scary and seldom explored second floor and out through the back door.

"What is it, Pete?" he exclaimed as soon as he was outside. "What is it?"

"Look out at the tracks. Look."

"Oh, wow," Frank rushed to Pete's side and excitedly grabbed his older brother's arm. "There must be a million of them."

"There sure is a lot. Must be a couple of hundred soldiers or more. And bunches of trucks. And jeeps."

"Tanks, too. Look at them, Pete."

"I see. Man, oh, man."

Frank jumped up and down gleefully. Some of the soldiers on the flat cars waved.

"Pete," Frank hollered, "they're waving at us. Hot darn."

"Wave back," Pete laughed. Frank flailed his arms.

For several minutes the boys watched the troop train roll slowly by. They didn't hear the back door open and close or their mother walk up a few feet behind them. The train continued on, rumbling through Jefferson, heading south.

"Pete," Frank finally asked, "where are they going? What are they all doing on that train?"

"I don't know," Pete said. "Maybe Camp Chaffee."

"Wow," Frank said, "all the way down there. Boy."

"I imagine they're going a good deal further than that, boys," Kate Mason said. The boys spun around.

"I didn't know you were out here, Mom," Pete said.

"I reckon not." Kate smiled. "You boys were so wrapped up in that train I'd a bit ya if I'd been a snake." Frank giggled. Kate rested her arm on his bony shoulders.

"Where do you think they're going, Mom?" Pete asked.

"I expect they'll be going on to the war," Kate replied.

"No kidding?" Frank asked.

"Like as not."

Frank jumped down into a crouch and went into a furious impression of soldiers in combat.

"I'm Johnny D.," he pointed an imaginary weapon at imaginary enemies, "take that and that. Bang. You're dead."

"Don't be disrespectful about Johnny Waters, son," Kate admonished her youngest.

He went on playing but not so loudly. The train continued on past. It stretched as far as you could see in either direction.

When Frank took his mock war a few steps away, Pete looked at his mother. "Mom, over there in the war is where Johnny D. got killed, wasn't it?"

"Yes, son, you know that."

"Why?"

"If I knew...well."

"Was he shot?"

"Yes. You remember I told you, don't you?"

"Yeah. He was shot a lot."

"Let's not dwell on it. Johnny's in a better place now. He was a good boy."

"Was he, Mom?"

"One of the finest."

"Did God want Johnny to die?" Pete asked.

Frank looked up from his game.

"Son, it's not that He wanted Johnny to die. It's just that Johnny had done what he was supposed to in this life. Then God took him away."

"Why?" Pete asked again.

"Why what?"

"Why did he have to die?"

"Don't be morbid, son. God works in strange ways. We may not always understand, but there's always a reason. Now, let's stop all this awful talk. Come on, Frank, we've still got some dishes to do. Pete, you come in right away, too. I've got to get ready for work."

"Okay, Mom," Pete said.

Kate headed back to the house, Frank clinging to her

skirt. Pete stayed in the back yard for the better part of a quarter hour, watching the rest of the train go by.

There were no more soldiers then, only vehicles and equipment. Everything was a dull green and without the men the train had lost most of its luster. At last the caboose came by, but Pete was so self-absorbed he didn't see the brakeman waving at him.

He thought of his lost cousin Johnny D. Waters, who he remembered as a short, square-shouldered boy from California. Johnny had teased the boys and bought everybody a strong smelling chunk of bologna. He gave Pete and Frank an amazing half-dollar apiece for spending. With the click-clack, click-clack of the train rapidly fading, Pete turned towards the house.

"I don't see any reason why he had to die," he said to himself, walking slowly to the back steps, "I don't see no reason for it at all."

God Is a Metaphor

Time from the beginning, time at the end;
Big Bang, Big Squeeze, eternity's dream.
Seek out answers where none exist;
invent some stories, write anything down.

Walk in a daze through time and space;
ask many questions, any answer will do.
How did it start, how will it end?
Answers don't matter if the questions are wrong.

Codify thought and constrain the mind;
write down nonsense as revelation or worse.
Search for something that cannot be found;
invent discoveries, make a wondrous show.

Mohammed, Buddha, Jesus and more;
Platonic images of Overlord or none.
Reach too far for a simple thing;
pull back complexity, empty out thought.

Face fear squarely, without crutch or cane;
choose reason and logic, the best that we have.
Let the loosened spirit sail and soar;
accept what's real—God is a metaphor.

Some Places We've Been

From the halls of Moctezuma
to Quaddafi's palace in Tripoli;
from the shores of little Grenada
to the bloody streets of Mogadishu—
these are some of the places we've been.

On the frozen soil of Mother Russia
and in the bays of hidden Japan;
on the tundra of Korean hill
and in the harbor at Vera Cruz—
these are some of the places we've been.

Off the coast of Cuba inventing the Maine
in the heart of Texas at the Alamo;
off the coast of Leyte and the Phillipines
in the belly of the hot and cold war beast—
these are some of the places we've been.

In a punitive search for Pancho Villa
a loud rock and roll grab of Noriega;

in a vaguely hidden displacement of Allende
a mostly forgotten disposal of Sandino—
these are some of the places we've been.
Insertions in the Dominican, Haiti, and El Salvador
assault in Guatemala for the sake of United Fruit;
insertions in Thailand, Laos, Cambodia, Viet Nam
assault on Indian, slave, the Spanish, the French—these
are some of the places we've been.

Occupy Germany, Afghanistan, Iraq and Japan
contemplate Iran, Kazahkstan, China and more;
occupy the homeland, the country, the state
contemplate the blueprint of tomorrow's new world—
these are some of the places we've been.

Blue Haze at Milepost 279

Blue haze at milepost 279
out from Los Angeles
on the highway
somewhere before Indio and Coachella
near old Desert Center
where the road once ran beside
mesquite, cholla, and Joshua Tree,
where the gas station, garage, and
greasy spoon sat at the turnoff to Needles
all changed now with smog rolling
down the empty interstate.

Desert Center mostly gone and near forgotten
like clear desert valley skies decades gone
gone with their bright, high washed out
blue clear palette – long miles then seeing
as far as the eye could wander
back to a time before sprawling air
floated out on wind, currents unknowing,
drifted out and away to become
blue haze at milepost 279
far from the toxic breath of city
far from the valley of angels
far from the distant, pristine past.

Your Poem (As If)

I carried around your poem
as if it were currency in some market of souls
as if having it would transform, create the past.
As if it could change me into something
I might not be.

I concealed it, hid it away,
away from those who would steal
what few hieroglyphs remain my own.

I guarded it, hoarded it, watched it,
watched it as if something would happen.
I watched it; I watch it still.

And it's still there, on some dusty shelf,
with the other relics of my life.
Nothing has happened, yet.
It hasn't changed,
it's just ink and paper—
it's still your poem.

Cadaver

Surprised, cadaver,
at how useless you've become?
Everything simply ended—
the guilt
the shame
the pride
the pleasure.

Everything.

Funny, isn't it, how quickly
it passed by?
How it was so good
   so bad
   so in between.
How you wanted so much and
could do so little.

Isn't it strange how you were
living, how you were?

And then it just ended.
In an instant. Without warning.

How was that, cadaver?
How could you be everything one moment
and nothing the next?

Why are you so silent there on the slab, cadaver,
did you lose your voice?
Where is your voice,
deep inside something, somewhere,
maybe/not isolated, alone,
screaming perhaps, crying why,
how, or maybe trying to tell us
what we will have to learn
ourselves?

Something Lost—A Night of Stars

Fifteen I stood there my friend
and I sharing my first—his who knew how many—
quart of beer
The grass was late spring dew wet
above the empty stadium
Here have a shot he said
Yeah drinking grimacing a throat full of bitter
Do you suppose there's life up there
And me looking up like some fool
saw stars cold far emptier than the stadium shivered
Do you think there's anything
No I said I don't know yes maybe
Scared like never before but many times since
Vision tunneled gut hurt fear frozen
God I said oh Jesus God
What's the matter he said
I said oh God no sense how can anything exist
What are you talking about
Oh Jesus it's nothing
Give the bottle here

Nothing
Oh shut up
Bowel moving skin biting hair electrifying
You don't understand nothin'
can't be nothing can it's not possible
Walked off in the dark with the bottle
Left alone not crying scared
with the black sky above—
Gone and gone just like that
beyond expression retelling.

December 1967

"Where's the scotch?" Butch asked above the blaring stereo.

"Ey?" Donner put a hand to his ear.

"The scotch."

Donner took a pipe from Jackson and pointed across the barracks room to Davis and Mason. Butch nodded and moved over behind them.

"I don't think I feel anything," Mason said.

"You will," Davis wiped off a record and slid it into its sleeve.

Mason took a deep drag from another pipe Davis handed him and held the smoke in as long as he could. He coughed and handed the pipe back. He lay flat of his back then, waving his arms to the music.

"Davis," Butch pleaded, "hand me that scotch, will you, dude?"

Davis handed it over. Butch moved back by Donner and Jackson. They were talking music.

"The Stones are best," Donner argued.

"Not anymore," Jackson said.

Jackson, a Californian, figured it was his duty to oppose

anything originating east of Laguna Beach. Donner, from New York, thought anybody west of Manhattan was an inbred hillbilly.

"C'mon, what about *Their Satanic Majesty's?*"

"What about *Sergeant Pepper* and *Magical Mystery Tour?*"

"What about all those Stones songs while The Beatles were makin' *Help*, huh?"

"That's yesterday. The Beatles are king again."

"Forget it, dude," Donner said, tiring of the argument. "Hey, Butch, gimme a hit of that scotch."

"You white boys fight over some seriously dumb crap," Butch laughed. He handed Donner the bottle.

Donner winked at Butch and chased a pipe hit with scotch. He handed the bottle over to Jackson. Jackson took a swig just as Mason popped up like a jack-in-the-box.

"What the hell?" Jackson almost choked.

"Oh, man, I can see it," Mason said. "Up, across, down. Ho, ho, ho, hee, hee, hee, ha, ha, ha. Like a line going up, across, and down. Cool."

"What are you talkin' about?" Butch shook his head.

"The Beatles," Mason mumbled. "They went ho, ho, ho, hee, hee, hee, ha, ha, ha."

"Lovely," Donner sniffed. "Real bright, Mason."

"And you ain't feelin' anything, right?" Davis joked. Everybody laughed.

"Oh," Mason lay back down. "After the Beatles," he muttered, "put on the Stones, 'Another Land.'"

"What?" Davis asked.

"He's out of it," Butch said.

"'Another Land,'" Mason repeated.

"He wants 'Another Land,'" Davis said to Butch.

"He's in another land," Donner laughed.

"We're all in another land," Butch joked, "this is North Carolina ain't it?"

Mason waved his arms around feebly.

"We'll play it, buddy boy," Donner told him. "You try to stay here in this land."

"Hey, Davis," Jackson said, "play the *Vanilla Fudge* album."

"Oh, come on," Donner moaned, "that's old crap."

"We still like it," Jackson said, pointing to the other guys.

"Yeah," Butch nodded at Mason, "but we gotta play the Stones for Mason."

"God," Donner laughed, "what a hick. These first-timers always overdo it."

Jackson reached one of the pipes across to Davis, who put on the song Mason wanted to hear. Mason made an unintelligible sound. Donner got the pipe from Davis, took another drag and offered it to Butch.

"You kidding," Butch said. "Smoke yourself to death if you want to. I'm gonna stick to scotch for a while."

"Suit yourself," Donner said.

On the floor, Mason continued to wave his arms weakly as if directing the music.

"Dum-ta-dum," he sang out loud, speech slow and slurred. "And the feathers floated by."

Davis looked at him and broke up laughing. Jackson and Donner resumed their Beatles/Rolling Stones argument. Butch clung to the scotch like it was the head of one of his opponents when he was an All Big-10 wrestler at Iowa. From his position just behind the others he watched with amused detachment.

"Jesus Christ," he said. Smoke and music blended with the buzz of conversation to give the airmen's room the atmosphere of an anonymous 1950's tea or coffee shop gone badly astray. "Look at these people, nothing but a bunch of potheads."

He took another drink of scotch and laughed. No one was paying any attention to him or anything else. They were all completely out of it.

Full Faded

False phallic home of glass and brick
rising vertical, past oak and elm
on ground once schoolyard spreading.

Near forgotten dreams, small memories
now late turned to crispen ash
and fading recollection some remembered.

Pre-death tomb of glass and brick
spreading horizontal, fronting street and house
on ground now home leading.

Long forgotten memory, small dreams
of late turned to wispen air
and lost recollection full faded.

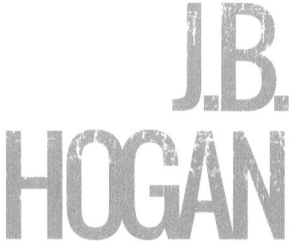

Merida

Ciudad gentil
   turistica
ciudad de arboles simetricos
   mendicantes ciegos, viejos.
Ciudad sorprendente
   verdusca
   madura.
Merida, ciudad Yucateca,
en la noche hay
   recorridos en los parques
   bailantes en las calles
   amantes en la sombra,
     oscura y viviente.

J.B. HOGAN

Merida
(Translation by Author)

Genteel city,
tourist city,
city of symmetrical trees,
of beggars blind, old.
Surprising city,
  lushly green,
  ripely mature.
Merida, Yucatan city,
in the night there are
  promenades in the parks
  dancers in the streets
  lovers in the shade,
    dark and vibrantly alive.

Political Sigh

Square Deal, New Deal, Fair Deal, no deal at all
plutocrat, technocrat, oligarchs, too;
affiliation, administration, accommodation to fools.

Bilateral, trilateral, reject Kyoto's Accord
Monroe, Truman, Marshall and more;
Lend Lease, Loose Lips, Sink Ships, war never ends.

Roosevelt, Roosevelt, Bush, Bush,
xenophobic, chauvinistic, jingoist toads;
MIA, KIA, Collateral Damage a modern term.

NATO, SEATO, UNICEF and WHO
IMF, World Bank, austerity plans;
Third World, Fifth World, poor poorer yet.

Ballot box, hanging chad, voter fraud's overt
horse race, beauty race, toss up for what?
Electoral College, Supreme Court, change the popular vote.

Nicaragua, Iran, Grenada, intervention's just fine
War on Poverty, War on Terror, on Drugs, and on Brains;
Korea, Viet Nam, Gulf Oil states,
Iraq and Iran for a thousand years.

Populist, communist, anti-nomian felon
Marxist, Leninist, Trotskyite, banished from thought;
Smith, Voodoo, Trickle Down to the parched below.

New Order, Old Order, once enlightened thought
modern wisdom inadequate at best;
political solutions, fought for and lost.

Old Hope, High Tech, modern jive
word on word, lexicon dry;
step back and breath, release a political sigh.

Ameca Ameca

Black smoke spewing bus clanking down from Mexico City
tourists and travelers climbing out into the central market
of Ameca Ameca, tiny green pueblito beneath
towering, dormant Ixtaccihuatl, and the pass
between Popocatepetl through which Cortez came
marching to Tenochtitlan to subdue mighty Moctezuma.
Tourists and travelers now, in peaceful, calm Ameca Ameca,
searching for a ganga, a bargain, a real deal.
A square-bottom summer shirt—cheap guayabera—
pulseras for the girlfriend's wrist,
a Phillies baseball cap marked down twenty percent.
Behind the central market, another mercado, inside,
short yards from the bus stop, with more shops
selling more clothes and trinkets,
and in back the butcher's shop with fresh
goat heads staring blankly from a counter,
chopped up limbs and entrails
of dead chickens, piled on a table,
bone and flesh runway for
buzzing fly and crawling bug.

Rest stop done, reboarding then,
turistas and travelers watch through
darkened windows of black smoke spewing bus
clanking its way out of little Ameca Ameca
rumbling down narrow road to lush Oaxaca,
its cool sensual evenings waiting, far from
the simple village beneath mighty Ixtaccihuatl,
between Popocatepetl and the far south,
quiet, unplumbed Ameca Ameca.

Mercado

Two nuns from South America, bags of pan de agua from a nearby panadería clutched under their arms, crossed a bustling street into the Rio Piedras mercado about two blocks east of the main University of Puerto Rico campus. Chugging, smoke-belching city buses rumbled down the loud, narrow streets toward the main local terminal north of the busy marketplace.

The nuns paused at an outer stall on the edge of the Mercado to haggle over the price of some late season cneppas, a grape-like fruit from the hilly countryside outside the capitol of San Juan. Suddenly a boy ran past them waving a long shiny switchblade knife.

He jostled one of the nuns, knocking the bread out of her hands. She looked up, angry at first then terrified, just as two uniformed policemen came in the back of the mercado.

Rushing by souvenir stores and rows of coffee bins filled with aromatic beans from Colombia, Nicaragua, and Cuba, the police drew their sidearms and fired at the retreating youth.

Amid the shouting and bedlam, the panicked boy ran headlong into a fish stall, spun around and froze. The policemen fired three times, hitting the boy in the chest twice. He fell backwards onto the chilled flesh and dirty ice of the stall, his knife clattered along the concrete floor of the *mercado*.

"He robbed the hamburger place by the university," one of the policemen explained to the bewildered crowd.

"He wouldn't stop," the other policeman said.

"He wouldn't stop," the first policeman repeated.

Some of the crowd gathered around the dead boy. They stared at his bleeding body lying there among the ice-covered fish. Blood drained onto the ice. The fish vendor tried to wipe it off with a soiled rag.

One of the policemen picked up the boy's knife and put it in his pocket. One of the South American nuns coughed, then turned and vomited onto the mercado floor. An old lady near her gagged. The fish vendor kept trying to wipe the blood off the fish.

There Are Buffalo

There are buffalo across the highway,
uphill by barbed wire fence,
winter scraggly beasts chasing a black pickup—
boy in back tossing bales of hay
onto last night's snow,
triangular white patch, bright against
washed out brown of a dead hay field.
And nearer, to the right, a jogging horse,
dark beside the barbed wire
of his separate, fenced off track;
disappearing then, behind weather-faded
wood shelters of ostriches—ostriches
tall, gangly birds
surely confused by cold and snow,
standing on tiptoe in closed, wire compound.
Across, then, further left on the hill,
dug out mounds of dirt and ice,
in one, the wreck of a caterpillar,
small, orange machine
half down in, half up out of, the hole—
metal treads stopped and rusting
jagged in the lead gray light.

Metamorphosize

Watery amniote to red-faced infant
dull caterpillar to winged beauty
cocoon state to external birth,
all begin, all change, metamorphosize.

Playful child to young adult
fresh bloom to seasoned maturity
rapid growth to static life,
all begin, all change, metamorphosize.

Mid-life toiler to reflective elder
incipient staleness to hoary wrinkle
ripeness of age to ultimate decline,
all begin, all change, metamorphosize.

Venerable guide to feeble ancient
weakened body to inevitable death
exhausted shell to forgotten dust
all begin, all change, metamorphosize.

Alien

Lying there beside you,
your warm legs across our distance,
    a distance so far;
you feel like an alien,
not wholly unfamiliar, yet different somehow,
as if you were from somewhere else,
    sometime long ago,
    someplace that maybe—
never was.

Gray Man

Gray man, simple man, empty man.
The color has all been drained from you;
no more plaids or useless rainbow flash,
no more flush of heat or excitement.

Drab man, basic man, hollow man.
The strength is gone, the fibre weak;
all burned to ash,
all hope reduced to memory.

Aging man, same man, cold man.
The blood thickens, the heart runs slow;
it can't be healed with a transplant,
cured with a transfusion,
it won't get better in time, won't be coming back.

Gray man, all man, senseless man.
The skin draws, discolors, blotches, rots;
no more chance for tomorrow, speculation, or reason,
no more to hold onto, to feel, to touch.

The Wind

In the short grass it lay,
still, breath stopped.

No sound, no motion,
only faint smell lingering—
pungent reminder of refuse.

The indifferent wind lifted,
spun odor on air,
scattering it afar.

In the short grass it lay;
still, breath stopped.

The wind, silent wind,
blew over, against it,
not lingering, not feeling,
unconcerned.

Corridors

Empty corridors, blue-lined
maze without purpose,
stretching out and across:
left, right, center.

Silent corridors, concrete-backed,
monolithic, stand inert,
appearing, seeming to move,
movement without energy or motion.

Blank corridors, primer gray,
giving away nothing at all
receiving nothing, stone lifeless,
perhaps come from dank woods or shining beach.

Tiring corridors, endlessly connecting,
escapes so few and futile,
relentlessly leading to the end of nowhere;
your impotence growing by the day.

Death corridors, mind smashing,
unrelated to blood, strain or twitch;
like a rune on straight razor edge
like a boulder seconds before toppling—
directly overhead.

Borinquen Exile

In Borinquen exile he sat,
thumbing through *Ulysses* like it was an article
in the *Reader's Digest*,
a cup of near-hemlock always at his side.

A learner not a teacher,
absorbing image and metaphor
like heat from the hot tropical sun that
poured from him like sweat,
silently burning off in a stinging mist.

Nothing gained, nothing lost,
just a chemical process to stay alive—
to continue an ancient quest,
the search for symbol and code.

Looking for a private Rosetta Stone—
one that would convert Joyce into clarity
hemlock into aged, smooth rum
and distant isolation into an image of community.

He Was Lying in a Hammock

He was lying in a mesh net hammock strung between two palm trees thinking about having a cold beer when he first spotted her. She came up Cielo Beach from his left, from down where a collection of bombed out tanks and trucks from old U.S. Navy shellings sat in rusting, eternal uselessness.

At first he thought he must be dreaming—surely she was only a vision, a play of heat and sun reflected on clear green water. Whether dream or illusion, he could tell by the way she walked that she was beautiful. Her hips swayed as she strolled along the white sand shoreline. Tiny waves lapped against her brown calves.

He watched her as if they were the only ones on Cielo Beach, on the island of San Mateo, on the entire planet itself. She came closer and turned up the beach towards him. He could see her clearly then and she was definitely beautiful.

She had athletic thighs, full hips, a thin waist, and flat stomach below breasts that swayed slightly beneath a thin blue T-shirt. She had smooth, fine features—high cheeks, a narrow slightly flat nose, and a full, gently curved mouth. Her dark brown eyes matched her hair, worn in a short, natural style.

He stared at her as she passed and for a moment she met his gaze. Her eyes flickered mild interest and a stronger amusement. It seemed as if she might laugh out loud.

He watched her walk away down the beach, sensuous buttocks straining against the tight cloth of her shorts, until she reached a campsite at the farthest end of the beach. The campsite was near a cove and promontory above which a full moon had begun to rise, promising a night of pure white light upon the restful shores of Cielo Beach.

He saw her join a group of several other young women and men. In the dying sunlight he could no longer see her distinctly. He forced his attention away, broke the dream-like spell.

He made himself think about having a beer. He envisioned a cold, refreshing bottle with water beads dripping down the side. Not the right image. Suddenly, impulsively, he rolled out of the hammock and instead of going for a beer ran stumbling to the shore. He flung himself into the waist-deep, pristine green waters.

He quickly came back up spitting. He pushed the hair out of his eyes. He'd forgotten the water was salty. No matter how long he lived in the islands, he always came up with a mouthful of salt water, gagging and sputtering brine. It was amazing he never seemed to remember where he was.

With a last glance down the beach to his left, he jogged out of the water laughing and splashing—and headed straight for the beer.

Gentle Day with Light Breeze

Gentle day with light breeze—
whispering leaves on Elm and Sycamore,
warm and sunny bright
a gentle day, and light.

Calm and safe day—
quiet, easy-going
no crowds, no clouds,
no loud or strident sound.

Pleasant day—
for reading, writing and such
a day without fear
no hunger, violence, or death.

Day of contentment—
of peaceful reflection and musing
without rancor or remorse
no past regret, no worrisome tomorrow.

Gentle day, rare and beautiful thing—
with life lived in the here and now,
in no other time, no other place,
only in this, this tranquil moment, caught forever
in the slow-running amber of time,
on a gentle day—with light breeze.

It Is

Divined more than thought
born outside tradition, never sought
not now new, nor without flaw
but no dogma, church or law
slow building, from empty feast
quiet building, without acolyte or priest
Greco-Latin of Plato and Rome
at last finding a world, a home.

Awareness on wind through eons fly
electric impulses in the nebula sky
hereafter forgotten, restful dark embrace
forgotten in memory, yet still a light space
fear then irrelevant, knowing is clear
peace then the object, irrelevant the fear.

Braceros

Beneath the desert sun they worked:
thin bodies bent double in dusty rows,
with bronzed and calloused hands,
thinning cotton with short-handled hoes.

Mid-morning sun, eye-burning, strength-sapping heat
rising in waves off the ground,
thinking of lunch time beans and tortillas,
jars of *jalapeños*, the afternoon ahead.

Working fiercely for a dollar an hour,
saving it for a cheap radio or new straw hat,
all else saved, hoarded, sent to family
in Hermosillo or Ciudad Obregón.

Below the scorching valley sun they worked,
tired bodies still strong, with discipline and pride,
doing what others would not, doing what was necessary,
for life, home, and family.

Chameleon Boy

How does it feel, chameleon boy,
to be dying?
Colors unneeded,
splotches considered a disease?

Blow up your throat sac,
do your electrical-jerky pushups;
push back from the end.

It's only fear, anger—
loss of identity,
continuing life in your absence
that rankles so.

Go ahead, regenerate yourself—or try,
make the colors change,
the cells grow anew.
Crawl along that thin limb
onto which you cling.

Do something.

Fall scale-shattering back to earth,
leave residue on a leaf,
slide around and beneath your tree.

Time is passing, chameleon boy,
make up your mind,
the waiting is tiresome.
Saggy skin is hardly a treat to anyone,
a lack of movement no excuse.

React will you?
Breath in, breath out,
or get out.

No one cares for a dramatic
final death scenc.

It's Not About Me

It's not about me, at least I've learned that much.
It's mostly on the outside, in the space
where everything else goes on as usual
without any need of an I or a me.

The trees and grass, high blue skies,
animals, humans, mighty nebula clouds,
spirits of energy floating here and there,
disease and pestilence, rotting, inevitable death—
none of that needs me.

It is definitely not about me.
I'm just an occupant, a walker on an erratic road,
trying to steer clear of disaster, to stay out of the way of trucks,
looking for a little pleasure, trying not to feast too much.

All of this is patently obvious, of course,
nothing more than a way of
showing how small one grain is on a sandy beach,
how infinitesimally small we look from a cosmic view.

So, it's not about me,

at least that much seems clear,

that much we know;

but don't get confused, here, or too filled up with yourself,

because the corollary is undeniable as well—it's not about you,

no, it's not about you either, not about you at all.

An Awesome Poet

You see, I'm this really awesome poet. I really know how to show people the real inner me. My mother says it's a gift, my calling. All I know is I've been through so much I'm overflowing with the need to tell everyone about my super special life.

My step-father says I haven't done anything or been anywhere, but what can you expect from an old insensitive hater. He doesn't understand me, doesn't get it all. How could he? He's old and irrelevant. A loser.

But I can't let that kind of negativity bring me down, man. I'm burning with this vision of the world. I'm unique, my girlfriend Maisie tells me, and she knows what's happening. I have to tell you about Maisie, what a thing we have going. I even write poems about it. I read one of them down at a local open mic program at a hip coffee house. I introduced all the locals to real slam poetry that night. Maisie was right there in front of me, giving me support and looking like the super-size babe she is. I read them this:

Nobody loves like we do, baby,
nobody knows how.
You're a full-figured mama
and I'm your daddy-man.
People don't understand us,
they don't get who we are.
We're red hot lovin' poets
and that's the way we roll.
When my great big man-ness
is all up against your fleshy self,
I'm all over you, baby,
Like a poet laureate in heat.
When we do it, mama,
it's epic and beyond the pale,
nobody does it like us, nobody
knows how, 'cause
we're the real deal, we're
flesh and blood, and juice and sinew,
we make love like no one else,
'cause you're my love-making sweet thing
and I'm your poem writing, loving man.

Oh, yeah, I really blew them away with that one. The crowd was stunned into silence by the power of my love. I'm not trying to be on some ego trip but I know I'm good and they do, too. It's who I am, it's how I project, man.

When I walked back to my seat, Maisie was all 'you knocked their socks off, baby' with me and we locked spitty lips right there in front of everyone to show them the depth of our love and how we're not ashamed to show it in public. If you got it, flaunt it. That's a philosophy I go with.

Later that night I read the poem to my mother and she was like really impressed and told me I had a real insight into life.

"Yeah, like I'm hip to that," I told her, thinking about some cool poets I'd read about.

They were these guys called Kershack and Ginseng or something like that I had heard somebody talk about who used to be big famous poets back a long time ago. I figured they were guys like me – really hip and way ahead of their time. We suffer a lot because we're so advanced from your average so and so person but it's what gives us our deep understanding of life and brings out the great poetry. Oh, yeah, I'm like those guys, man, exactly like them.

After my great night at the coffee house, I decided to write another poem. I was really on a roll now. I was burning with poetry. I told Maisie to meet me at the coffee house again like before and that I had a big surprise for her this time, even bigger than the surprise of my poem about our physical and spiritual love.

Before I took off I read the poem to my mother, even though my hater step-dad insisted on listening to it, too. Naturally, my mother knew it was great but the old man started laughing right away and didn't stop until I finished reading. What a jerk. And then he had the nerve to tell me my poem stunk. What could he know? He was just an old turd who never had a life and was taking it out on everyone around him. Artists like me have to deal with people like that all the time.

I had to wait nearly an hour before I went on, but Maisie and I sat there necking off and on and making fun of the lousy poets ahead of me. Finally it was my turn to get up. I gave Maisie a load of tongue and spit and headed up to read.

"'They Don't Get It' is the name of my poem," I told the crowd. "I think you'll maybe get it."

> *How can I tell you*
> *how hard it is to live at home*
> *with parents who don't get you?*
> *Can you really feel my pain?*
> *Do you know how hard it is?*
> *I'm creative, man, I need space*
> *to grow and be great.*
> *How can you know what it is*
> *to be an artist, and misunderstood.*
> *Only my loving girlfriend knows,*
> *only she appreciates the depth of my angst.*
> *Oh, life is so hard for the true poet,*
> *living in a world so cruel and unconcerned.*
> *Better that life should end early*
> *than go through the hell of un-appreciation*
> *and the agony of being ignored.*

Well, when I finished a couple of people applauded. They got it. But a couple of old farts pinned me next to a coffee machine and started putting me down. They were obviously unhip, local nobodies. I told them where to get off and stormed out.

I could hear laughter as I left but I didn't care. I'd show them. I'd go home and write a poem about haters like they were. I'd even name the poem that. Yeah, that's a great title:

"Hater's Hating on Me." Perfect. It'll practically write itself. That'll show everyone my talent, how deep and significant I am as a poet. You bet it will. They'll all come to understand: I am an awesome poet.

Reservation

Driving through outdoor ghetto of
empty bottles, strewn trash, people collected by store.
Scraps of paper, torn and white, drift, float, and litter.

Haunted reservation, memory cut off, two-thirds lost,
Haunted by phantom riders roaming far on grassy slope
    by sharp, clear morning and easy star-filled night
    by denial, fast, and vision.

Dying reservation, dreams with no more life,
dying from fence, machine, and road
    from imprisoning isolation and untouchable expanse
    from indulgence, excess, and despair.

Looking at tenements of trailer and mud
scattered cans, dumped garbage, families by communal stove
wisps of smoke, pungent and blue, rising, drifting—away.

Away from reservation
    from spirit, dream, and fire
    to fence, ghost, and death.

Nothing Up Ahead

The long road, once beckoning
Now shortened, cut back
No more twists, nor turns left

The early dream, once waiting
Now past, far behind
No more visions, nor pictures left

The budding hope, once growing
Now shriveled, drawn back
No more wishes, nor desire left

The imagined life, once expanding
Now closed, doors shut
No more chances, nor opportunities left

The sweetest love, once warming
Now cold, dead cold
No more caresses, nor affection left

The final act, once denying
Now accepted, endgame done
No more breath, nor living left.

Pre-Dawn Gray

In the pre-dawn gray,
the station, dusty and decaying,
waits mutely in the chill desert air.

In the distance, a train,
rigid metal arrow,
pierces the heart of the fertile valley
and is impelled on,
on toward those who wait.

Signaling out its path with a melancholy whistle
that echoes over winter green fields
like the moan of wind on wire
it comes at last to a sighing stop.

Sighing, those who have waited step forward
to claim flag-draped boxes—
or to receive flags folded, triangled, presented.

Then, in the cool light of dawn,

the valley stirs, awakens,

and the train lurches forward,

rumbles on, metal on metal,

across desert, plain, to city,

its harsh metallic whistle sounding through the land

like a chill wind, sharp and unseen,

echoing down some long, cold wire

in the distance.

Forgotten Pages

Long, full shelves
stretch back and up, across.
Hidden gold pages
ancient, water-stained marks.

Home now to cobwebs,
dusty termites and ageless dust.
Once finger-oil shiny,
given way to marked disuse.

Backs chipped and grimy,
creak when opened or shut.
Colors nearly faded out
letters once black, gone to a vague gray.

These long shelves
stretch up and back, across.
Isolated, forgotten pages
with ancient, golden marks.

They are waiting, waiting
waiting even for the echo
of some rare, unexpected heel on marble
the unlikely anticipation of touch and opening,
the thrill and shock—of removal.

Holy Leper

And you, holy leper,
can you swear it was I
and not you who refused to enter
the area of the diseased,
or did you leave me outside of your own accord?

There I sat
in the cold, wet grass,
my pants stained—
one moment I was looking at the sky
awestruck, fearful, reverent. Hopeful?
Christ, I was only a kid,
and then you were gone.

I was looking up at the sky
and the stars receded—pulled away.
It was cold, they receded,
I was looking up,
and then you were gone.
I sat there waiting.

Waiting. For what?

The sky was still, you were mute.

Christ, I was only a kid.

The stars were cold and you were still.

I expected more, and you were still.

And then you left,

left me waiting, waiting—

I am waiting still.

Wind Turbines—Eastern New Mexico

It looked like a long, jagged scar
twisting across the eastern New Mexico desert
an old cut, long healed but
ragged and angled into a half-moon.

From 34,000 feet that was impressive enough
but sitting on top of the dirt brown earth scar
were two dozen of those new wind turbines,
the kind they use to generate electricity
like in that gigantic field north of Palm Springs.

And the windmills were turning—
you had to concentrate to see the movement
but they were turning, turning
building up power for some city,
there was none in sight,
maybe Albuquerque or Santa Fe.

And the big propellers spun steadily, smoothly
sitting on top of that land scar in the brown,
empty New Mexico landscape,
going round and round
making electricity for somebody down there,
somebody who might not even know
the wind mills even existed, probably would never know
unless by accident they flew over them and looked down,
by accident, and saw a couple dozen wind turbines
spinning round and round on top
of a brown land scar in the vast
uninhabited eastern New Mexico desert.

Hemingway Hotel

Outside a second floor room
at an Ernest Hemingway hotel
there was beer, gin and tonic and,
inside, when the water pressure fell,
no showers.

Meals were taken below, by the kitchen—
brown beans and rice, or *mofongo con caldo*—
and around in front, at the tiny bar,
the next round always waiting.

Sometimes there were hitched rides to Flamenco Beach,
one hundred yards into waist deep, clear green water
in a cove on this *Culebra*, this snake island.

On the beach, an island girl browner than the sand,
locals bareback on horses—hooves splashing mist in the air;
on the promontory across the bay, a Navy lookout tower,
and on Saturday nights, Methodists parading in the streets.

Each morning dawned to crowing roosters—
one here, another there,
a contest, a celebration of a new day alive.
All heard and seen from a second floor room,
at an Ernest Hemingway hotel.

Hemingway Hotel

"What do you think, Juan," Dan McGuire peered into the shaded, open air bar of the Hotel Criollo on the little island of San Mateo, "do we get to the hotel through here?"

"Ask the man at the bar," Juan said, "I'll wait here with the *mujeres.*"

"Okay." Dan walked into the bar.

It was a quaint place, walls decorated with worn posters advertising cock fights from a distant past and faded displays for several domestic and imported beers. Some of them looked like they might have gone back to the 1940's.

"Bueno dia," Dan said to the bartender. He dropped the ending 's' in imitation of the locals.

"Bueno dia," the bartender looked up from drying a glass with a semi-clean bar towel.

"Uh," Dan motioned with his arm, "uh, *donde esta el* Hotel Criollo? *Es . . . esta cerca? De aqui?"*

"Si, Señor," the bartender switched to a heavily accented English in response to Dan's weak Spanish.

"The hotel is back *alla,* back there" —he pointed down the open side of the bar and then to the right behind it— "back there is the manager."

"Oh good, that's great. Gracia, Señor. Mucha gracia."

The bartender nodded and went back to his work. Dan rejoined Juan and their girlfriends, Gabi Solis and Susan Hart.

"This is it." Dan said as they collected their gear. "We have to go by the bar and around behind it. The guy in there said the manager's in back somewhere."

The manager, a thin, voluble man of perhaps forty-five, was in fact in a small dining and kitchen area just around and behind the back wall of the bar.

"Welcome," he greeted the new guests enthusiastically, "welcome to the Criollo. It is a nice view of Edison from the second floor."

He led the group upstairs to their rooms, chatting pleasantly in imprecise but adequate English.

"You can see nearly to the ocean. A very nice view."

"It is a beautiful view," Gabi looked out at the white stucco houses dotting the green hillside beyond.

"Can we eat downstairs?" Susan asked.

"*Si, señorita.* We open for lunch and dinner. We have much good food. My girlfriend is the cook." The manager laughed, revealing a set of well-shaped, clean white teeth.

"And the *playa,"* Juan asked, "how do we get there?"

"People go often to Cielo Beach," the manager said. "You can catch a ride with anyone going there or my men Victor or Luis will take you. Come with me, *señor*, one of them is maybe in the bar now." He and Juan started down the stairs.

"Oh, yes," the manager paused a couple of steps below the landing. "I nearly forget. The water pump is not so good. Sometimes the... uh, pressure is low and there is no water. Mostly in the afternoon, when the people come back from the beach. I am sorry."

"No problem," Gabi said. "We don't mind. It'll be fun, huh, Dan?"

"You bet," Dan said, "no problem." He had checked out the room while the others visited.

"Good," the manager said, pleased. He motioned to Juan and they hustled off to the kitchen/bar area.

"God, you guys," Dan happily told the women. "Check this place out. The bar, that little dining area. This is like something out of Hemingway, isn't it? Man, it makes you want to pull up a table and chair on this landing, grab a cool one, and write all day. Whew! What a place! I could spend some time here, let me tell you."

—

"I could've stayed there forever," Gabi said as the couples climbed the Criollo's stairs. "I didn't want to leave."

"Me either," Susan said, "Cielo Beach is the most beautiful beach I've ever seen in my life."

"You can say that again," Dan confirmed.

"Con permiso," an old man said from the top of the stairs.

He and another man of similar age came down the stairs just as the two couples neared the landing. Dan and the others moved to one side.

"Con su permiso," the man repeated, more firmly, more formally.

He wore a red *guayabera* shirt, white beach pants and black flip-flops. He was clean shaven, with steel black hair dotted with an occasional speck of white. He had dark brown eyes and laugh wrinkles around his eyes. The other man wore a spotless white *guayabera*. He was balding and had not shaven. He nodded to the group and made his way down the stairs.

"Wasn't it fabulous," Susan picked up the conversation when the men had passed.

"Better than St. John's?" Juan asked.

"I don't know," Susan said, "maybe. In its own way."

"Listen," Dan said, "let's hurry up and if we can, get some dinner downstairs, okay? I'm starving and I love that little place down by the bar."

"I know, I know," Gabi laughed, "it's so Hemingway."

—

Juan and Dan were drinking and getting a little boisterous at a table out on the second floor landing when the two older men who had passed them on the stairway earlier came out of their room across the way.

"Buenas noches," the dark-haired man extended a hand in greeting. He held a bottle of rum in the other. "I am Jorge Ruiz and this," he added in English, pointing to the other man, "is David Lopez. May we join you and share our drinks?"

Dan and Juan shook hands with the older men and invited them to sit down.

"So," Jorge said, after the preliminary courtesies were exchanged and a round of straight rum poured, "we heard much loud talking before. What was it about? Mujeres?"

"No," Juan laughed, *"yanquis.* We were saying how much they control things on the main island."

"The Yankees," Jorge pretended to misunderstand, "what has a New York baseball team to do with controlling Boca Tierra?"

"Estupido," David, already clearly in his cups, grumbled, "not those Yankees, the other *yanquis."*

"Oh," Jorge acted surprised by his friend's response, "oh." Juan and Dan laughed courteously.

David refilled the glasses. He spilled some on the table and cursed. Juan and Dan glanced at each other. Jorge hurriedly mopped up the alcohol with a handkerchief.

"Say," he proposed, "would everyone like a game of dominoes?"

"Sure," Juan and Dan shrugged.

Jorge hustled off, shortly returning with the dominoes. In moments the game was in full swing and Susan and Gabi came out to watch the spirited play. There was a lot of laughing, loud talk, and drinking.

Jorge and David consistently overwhelmed Dan and Juan. Juan managed to hold his own but Dan couldn't keep up. They were always handily beaten. Jorge took each victory in stride, insisting that Juan and Dan were improving every game and that Dan was really catching on fast.

David, whose sullenness intensified as the games mounted up, was not so generous. Around eleven, with the game and energy of the drinkers winding down, the sullenness slid toward open hostility.

"Wonderful move, amigo," he growled at Dan after a particularly inept play. "Done like a true yanqui."

"David," Jorge said, "shush. You are drunk. Don't insult our friends."

"Friends?" David snorted, his quick anger catching everyone off guard. "*Mierda*. Crap."

"*Ay bendito,*" Jorge told him. "You do this every time you drink. Must you?"

"Must you?" David mocked.

Juan and Dan looked at each other and at the girls. Jorge rolled his eyes in commiseration. Dan smiled at him.

"I'm tired of them being here," David started up again. "I'm sick of you *yanquis.*"

"*Por cierto,*" Juan tried to joke with him. "Let's chase them all out. Beginning with this one." He acted like he was grabbing Dan, who feigned fear.

"No," David slurred, first to Juan and then to Dan, "don't laugh. It is not a joke. I am sick to the death of yanquis. To hell with them. To hell with you all."

Juan's eyes flashed. Susan quickly put her hand on his shoulder.

"I am sorry friends," Jorge interceded again, "David is drunk. He is troubled and angry. Not at you personally, I assure you. He is not like this usually. It is a private thing."

"*Calleté,* Jorge," David butted in, "shut up. What do you know? For a hundred years they come here. They own everything. They steal our language, our religion, everything. All they do is take... take. Everything. I hate them."

"These people are not like that, David," Jorge said, "please be quiet."

"Oppressors," David said.

"I'm not like that, David," Dan said, "none of us here is. We don't believe like that. We hate that, really."

"You are all the same," David said, the fire as suddenly going out of his drunken harangue as it had flamed. "You are *yanquis,*" he mumbled sadly, "the women too."

"David!" Jorge said. "Now you must apologize."

"Yes," Juan rose to his feet, "apologize to my friends. And to my girlfriend."

"Juan." Susan reached out. "Come on. He's drunk. He didn't mean it. Let's go. Come on."

"Yeah, Juan," Gabi said, "forget it."

"Just watch what you say," Juan said to David. Jorge put his arms around his slumping friend.

"He is sorry, young man," Jorge told Juan, "even though he doesn't know it. Please forgive us. I'll take him to his room. We're sorry."

As Jorge helped David to his feet, he spoke softly to the couples.

"It is his son. A boy of about your ages. He was shot in the war in the Gulf. The right arm was taken and now the boy has many problems. It has broken David's heart. Please understand."

"Oh," Juan said, "I didn't know."

"No, of course not," Jorge told him. "How could you."

"We're sorry," Dan said.

"Thank you," Jorge said. "I will take him to the room now."

He guided David across the landing, leaving the dominoes and the rest of their rum. Susan noticed and picked up the table.

"We can give these to them in the morning," she said. "When everyone's sober."

"Let's go to bed," Gabi said. "I feel lousy."

"Yeah," Dan said, "what a drag."

"What do you think of your Hemingway hotel now?" Gabi asked him.

"I don't know," Dan said, "I was just saying that before. You know."

"I know," she said, taking his hand, "it's just that this is the kind of weird scene machismo and drinking always end up in."

"Not always," Dan said, as the couples entered their room.

"How would your Hemingway have handled this?" Juan sat down on the edge of one of the beds.

"Who knows, Juan," Dan answered, "probably about the same as us."

"Then he wouldn't have done a very good job of it, would he?" Gabi said.

"Let's go to bed," Susan said, "and forget Hemingway. He's long gone anyway."

"Right," Gabi said.

Juan let himself fall backward on top of the covers. Susan lay down beside him. Gabi sat on the other bed and motioned for Dan. He slowly walked over and sat beside her. In a moment, he too stretched out on the covers and closed his eyes.

"About the same as us, I guess," he mumbled.

"What?" Gabi asked, rolling over against him. He didn't speak right away.

"Uh... nothing," he finally said quietly, "nothing, nothing at all."

Blind Kid's Cry

Blind kid's cry
plaintive, fearful, full of need
raw-nerved, begging for attention
for help, for love.

Blind kid's cry
sharp announcement of life
unambiguous declaration of its presence
its will to live, its profound self.

Blind kid's cry
born of hunger, pain, terror
ear-piercing wish for life
for mercy, for care.

Blind kid's cry
undiminished demand to live
undiminished life force
its essence caught in
that terrible moment,
that terrible sound of insistent life
in the unavoidable bleating
of a blind kid's cry.

Yellow Aspen Leaves

Yellow aspen leaves float on
wind swirling down to
brown grass by clear-running creek—
fall spinning in widening spirals
dropping to green grass above the bank
in an inverted rustling imitation thermal
landing in thick quick-soaking patches,
covering the expectant ground.

Collecting now in soft-running stream,
thick with fall runoff overladen,
caught in bends by craggy rock and limb
some unbroken broken loose to float
swirling away downstream
past dying reed and rusted can,
by leaf-covered playground of wished for sand,
silent playground, all movement stopped—
empty, silent, and unmoving.

Big Houses

Between a small silo cylinder and a dead winter tree
there are three really big houses on the hill
all houses big, modern big, mansion big,
for what people?

Are they like me?
Do you suppose they're like me at all—
carbon-based, bipedal, oxygen breathers—
can those people in those great houses be like me?
I don't want to live in a huge house like that,
I want a little one room cabin off by a creek somewhere.

Do you suppose they're like me, though,
that there's someone up in a room on a top floor
looking out this way past a dead winter tree
and silo cylinder
looking at my little apartment, thinking:
do you suppose those people are like me—
omnivores, made up mostly of water,
walking upright against gravity—
can those people be like me?

Decade

Through the empty dirt lot
by the plant he walked,
towards the quiet street
and the cemetery beyond.

Above, in the deep, blue sky,
the white trail of a jet, silent, lengthened,
passed overhead, then drifted into
the distance of the new decade.

In the still, morning air,
in the trees beyond the railroad tracks he walked,
the cry of doves surprising
with their echo of his mute pain.

Stiff-legged, funereal, he reluctantly walked,
along the tracks, a victim
of perpetual movement,
finding that in either direction
the iron path had no bounds
and that whatever choice he made
would be no decision at all.

Your Dewy Throne

You sit upon your dewy throne
Its beauty to conceal
From many insistent courtiers
Who before you scrape and kneel

You broach no threat nor plea
From beggar, king or fool
You strive for one thing only:
Protect your fecund jewel

In youth your verdant trophy
Was sought by many men
One once won but then betrayed
Your priceless innocence

All changed then as seasons do
From summer sun to autumn chill
Your fertile seat shrank and froze
Though your heart it did beat still

None were allowed into the place
Where you kept your unattainable prize
You fended off all who would
Your unassailable walls circumscribe

But time will come and time will go
Your monarchy to barren waste decline
Fewer there to worship now
At your altar so fresh once and fine

Your lush soil brown dry will grow
Your tenderness crisp and sear
Until you walk alone in an empty land
Love's possibility your only fear.

Janey

When they first brought her down from the city, they became minor celebrities. The guys with the New York babe staying at their place. Melvin and Donny went into Manhattan from Melvin's home in Connecticut and saw the girl cruising around Washington Square Park completely stoned, dressed like a modern-day hippie.

She smiled sweetly at Donny and he wanted to make a move right then, but Melvin wanted to check out all the people in the park. Musicians played everywhere and a huge black man explained some law of spheres or something to a bored-looking businessman. Melvin and Donny hung around until they tired of being panhandled by everyone in sight, including the musicians.

Washington Square was like a zoo or the fair—funky people everywhere. Some guy tried to get a special view by stretching out on the grass in front of a girl in a short skirt. A wild-haired dude in cut-offs and T-shirt read poems about the holocaust. Lots of people were high. Melvin and Donny started to leave when the girl showed up again.

"Hey, guys," she put an index finger in her mouth all sexy like.

"What's up?" Donny leered at her.

"Maybe you," the girl laughed.

Melvin saw from her eyes that the girl was totally fucked up on something. It wasn't no weed either.

"Think so?" Donny put his hand on the girl's arm. She reached down between his legs.

"Do you both for something to eat," she firmly latched onto Donny.

"Uh," he half-moaned, half-grunted.

"What about you big man?" she said to Melvin.

"I'm game," Melvin said, totally ignoring the fact that he was planning to get engaged to his Connecticut girlfriend sometime really soon.

"Let's go," the girl told them.

"Oh, yeah," Donny followed her unyielding grip.

"Let's do it," Melvin shrugged.

All the freaks in the park would have to wait. This girl took precedence. She wasn't half bad looking either.

She took them to a toilet at one end of the park and afterwards they bought her a couple of slices of pizza at a little joint nearby.

"Why don't you come with us," Donny suggested after the chow.

"Where you goin'?"

"North Carolina," Donny said.

"Why not, I got no reason to be here."

"You're all about freedom, aren't you?" Melvin asked.

"How'd you guess, big man."

"I'm Melvin. That's Donny."

"I'm Janey. Pleased to meet you."

Back in Carolina, Melvin and Donny set Janey up in their off-base apartment and left her there while they went back on duty. Every day at noon, one of them made a quick run off base, bought her some fast food and tossed it in the door like she was an animal caged in a zoo. She didn't seem to care. She had a stash of pills she popped regularly and seemed to be content lying around the joint doing nothing.

In a few days, though, the place filled with garbage and stunk pretty bad. Not that Melvin and Donny gave a damn. The girl put out and that was good enough for them. Pretty soon they got bored with her and let their buddies take the food to her or come over at night and do it with her. In no time she'd done most of the guys from the headquarters unit.

Finally, after about ten days of living in that human dump and being abused steadily, the girl decided it would be better to go back home to New York. At first, Melvin and Donny resisted the idea, but she threatened to call the base and rat them out.

"Oh, no," Melvin held his hands up in surrender, "don't do that. That's not a good thing."

"Then get me a ticket out of this place," the girl demanded. "I'm tired of all your sick perv buddies coming in here and jumpin' on me. The crap you bring me to eat sucks, too."

"Come on, Janey," Donny cajoled, "it ain't that bad here."

"I'm out of my prescription."

"What prescription?" Melvin asked.

"Oxycotin," Janey held up her nearly empty bottle.

"We can't get that shit," Melvin told her.

"Hell, no," Donny said, "we'll get drummed out for trying to get that junk."

"Get me a ticket," Janey said simply.

Donny and Melvin scrounged up enough dough from their own meager pay and with the help of a couple of their friends bought the girl a ticket and put her on a bus for New York.

"It's been real," she said, climbing on the bus.

"Yeah," Donny said, "very real."

After the bus pulled out, Donny and Melvin sighed and laughed out the nervous tension. They never heard from Janey again but they didn't soon forget her.

Sick call the following week was overrun with guys complaining of a burning sensation when they urinated, including Donny and Melvin. Janey had gone back to New York, all right, but she left the boys from the base a little present to remember her by, a particularly virulent, not easy to treat STD. It was the last time the boys went searching for good times up in New York. Things were simpler down in North Carolina, lots simpler.

A Form of Ashes

Like a fiery carcinoma it spread,
burning anything in its way,
drying up sources and reservoirs.

Down from above it came,
from the top, the very gray top;
its stench barely confined,
its flames scarcely contained.

Then further down it slid,
down the ragged bony lengths,
separating, dissolving,
rending cartilage, nerve, and fat.

Until at last,
it reached out, pulling, claw-like, scorching
to the extremities themselves—
leaving in its aftermath a form of ashes,
an outline of what once had been,
a skeleton of lost potential
its life cavities great empty holes,
all fluids dissipated, their origins evaporated,
long eons now forgotten.

Half-Century Beats

Like Ferlinghetti of old, I am waiting, too.
And same as Johnny Nolan and Wilfred Funk
I have a patch on my ass, and
I am waiting for Jack Kerouac to come back,
with Ginsberg and Cassaday to City Lights.

I am still waiting, sort of, for:
"someone to really discover America...
the Second Coming...
the Salvation Army to take over."

And I am waiting for:
Christians and Jews and Muslims to convert to Buddhism,
people to stop believing anyway,
religion to just go away.

And I am waiting for:
newspapers to print the truth again,
the evening news to broadcast the truth again,
somebody to tell the Emperor he has no clothes.

And I am waiting for:
hacks to stop writing,
hacks to stop singing,
McGuane to keep writing.

And I am waiting for:
Jimmie Dale Gilmore to be elected president,
for Angelina, Ann, and Elton to be legally married,
and for whiners and complainers like me to shut up.

And I am waiting for:
this poem to stop
but it can't—
because there's no end in sight
the waiting never ends—it never will.

Jacky Kerwacky Ridin' the 242

Jacky Kerwacky ridin' the 242
down to Mexico City, man.
Be boppin' for Buddha, Tathagata,
maybe Ferdinand the Bull.
Or maybe findin' Quetzalcoatl—
Kate-sol-co-ott-el—or blind flippin' ecstasy
just off the gray concrete of the zocalo,
blowin' long blues back to Midwest afternoons,
into Midwest minds hopin' to escape,
lookin' for how it should go
tryin' it on for size
catchin' that last shot and givin' it a pop—
a pop, a bang,
a "how's that for an ending, huh?"

All from Jacky Kerwacky
all from 242
all osmosified, transfigurized,
in a kerplunkerous gelatinous sea
of rotgut hogshine

of portotooty death, baby,
while you waitin' to get free
of that meat wheel grinder and
up to nowhere land where you are safely
never dead.

Hitching Out

Early February, Twenty Above

Twenty above, standing by the Higginsville exit, two onion and cheese sandwiches apiece and five dollars between them. A girlfriend's car disappearing down Highway 13 like the last link to safety and comfort, which it was.

It was cold on the highway but they only had to wait a little over an hour for the first ride. It was a perfume salesman. His car was soft and warm inside and had a strong feminine odor. He talked about his job, how he traveled, some of the fascinating people he met, how young people were really okay by him.

But he only went to Kansas City and dropped them off on I-70 just before the road turned north to loop around town and head on to St. Joseph. They reluctantly went back into the cold, the buildings of downtown looming up in the background, gray, impersonal, unconcerned. The perfume salesman gave each of them a bottle of cheap cologne and they stowed them in their bags wishing it had been something warm to eat or drink. It was still morning.

"Hey, white boys," the girl called. "Hey, you need a ride?"

They hustled down the embankment to the waiting car, a long, white Pontiac. There were three girls, two skinny and one fat, and one guy – a totally nodded out doper. They were going to Denver.

At any speed the car weaved and floated from side to side, scaring the hell out of them. As soon as they crossed the state line into Kansas one of the tall skinny girls took the wheel, put the Pontiac at about 120 mph and left it there.

The car sailed, literally sailed down the interstate and the girls started talking about shooting smack and began harassing the stoned out dude. They were kind of bitchy girls and one time they put a match into the guy's face and burned some of his beard. It smelled awful but didn't seem to bother him. He was definitely gone.

Somewhere past Lawrence they stopped for gas and the girl driving decided it would be a good idea to just pull right away without paying. Take off without removing the gas hose from the tank. At the last minute she changed her mind and paid the bill. At that point, the hitchhikers were convinced weaving back and forth down the interstate at 100 plus wasn't so bad after all. At least there weren't cops after them, too. It was a relative sort of thing.

An hour or so later, the skinny girl driver suddenly pulled over onto the shoulder of the road and announced that they were turning back for Kansas City. The two hitchhikers were presently in the absolute middle of nowhere.

"This is it," the girl said.

"We gotta go back," the other skinny girl said.

"Yeah, we have to," the dude said.

"Shut up," the fat girl told him. She hit him on the arm. He stared off into space.

The hitchhikers climbed out. It was the warmest part of the day. It still felt cold as hell to them.

"They won't be goin' back to Kansas City," one of them said, watching the Pontiac fade into the horizon.

"No," the other one said.

"They dumped us 'cause we didn't have dope."

"Think so?"

"Yeah, the main driver girl was mad about that. I heard her say it at the station back there."

"We're probably better off."

"I suppose. But this sure as hell ain't nowhere."

"No."

"This is Kansas."

"Exactly."

"Let's eat one of the sandwiches."

"Good idea."

A Nice Farm Girl

She was a nice farm girl and she took them all the way to Hays. By then it was getting late and the temperature was dropping faster than their spirits.

"You boys know how to read?" the highway patrolman gruffly asked. He was about ready to kick their cans into storage for a few days, but they didn't give him any grief and they were clean—their Federal and Kansas records that is.

"You can't stand up here on the highway," he said. "You'll have to wait off the highway by the entrance ramp. Before it. You can't be a traffic hazard. Clear?"

Clear. They walked down to the bottom of the ramp and waited. It was beginning to get real cold. The sun was almost gone.

Another hitchhiker talked to them a while. He said somebody had taken a shot at him somewhere this side of St. Louis. Probably didn't like people bumming rides. Sometimes, he said, he went to airports and hitched rides on private planes. They weren't exactly sure about that one.

Then the sun went down. They started pacing. Back and forth. Back and forth. It was very dark. It was very cold.

This Girl Was Very Young

This girl was very young and very pretty and drove a yellow Plymouth. At first they were so warm they both fell asleep. Later they shared the driving but finally had to stop and let everyone sleep for a while.

They reached the outskirts of Denver while it was still dark but beginning to lighten up. On the way to Boulder, the girl told them she was sixteen, from San Diego, and that she had stolen the Plymouth from her dad and just taken off. They looked at each other and shook their heads.

When they got to Boulder it was gray, light, but no sun

yet. The mountains pierced the sky beyond the town and hung there, dominant, oppressive.

"I'm going on to California maybe later today or tomorrow," the girl said. "Meet me at the CU union or be around there and I'll look for you. I got people here. I want to visit them."

"Us too," one of them told her. "Maybe we'll see you later."

"You serious," the other one said when the girl was gone, "go on to California? I thought this was where we were going."

"You're right."

"Forget California."

"Yeah, forget it. There's millions of people out here. We can find a place to crash."

"Alright, then, we made it."

"Let's get something to eat."

"I'm for that."

"Later we look for something to do."

"And a place to crash."

"Right on."

They walked into a small, early-hours cafe and ordered eggs, potatoes, toast, and coffee. Outside they could feel the presence of the mountains, cold, powerful, unconcerned. They'd gone as far as they were going. They didn't think about the pretty, under-aged girl in her daddy's stolen car, or California. They'd give Colorado a run for the money. That's what they intended to do anyway.

The Plague

The plague should have buried you
in the mass graves of the unsaved dead
denied final absolution by your philosophy.
What better proof that your myths were
so much pestilent air like the
green miasma of the great death itself.

Who else to blame but pagans, whores,
the offal- and pustule-covered sinners themselves,
no monarch could be responsible,
no cowardly priest—nor the quivering, hidden father,
face glowing from the high flames
burning before his holy desk.

Sin brought God's vaporous retribution
not filth, stupidity, or epidemic.
Man born, man borne, one in three dead, or worse
one-half of poor Siena, millions upon millions more,
and sorrowful Edward's lost, dear Joanna.

In the streets of Freiburg, flagellants parade,
cheering, worshipping, their excess turned
to condemnation, to heresy—more fuel
for inquisition fires.

Finally spent, death at last relents
the stench rolls back, the air cleans—
revealing mass grave upon mass grave
throughout the exhausted land.

Safe again, all scurry about once more,
worker, lord, burgher and priest, order saved, restored.
Reborn in the triumph of irrationality,
rebuilding upon untold heaps of untold, unclean dead,
dead from the black death,
the plague that should have buried you beneath it,
buried you for all time.

Thomas Wolfe Saw James Joyce

On the tour bus from Brussels he sat in back
sizing up the Irishman's skinny face,
remembering old days at Harvard and
the illegal copy of Ulysses when
he imagined himself to be the equal
of the eternal Gaelic expatriate
with his cool, aloof bearing
and single black eye patch
beneath cheap wire spectacles.

At Waterloo, the son, Giorgio was friendly,
conversant, but the wife and girl ignored him,
as did Joyce, though he saw the good eye
size him up more than once.

On the way back, he sat behind again,
still not introduced, still not talking,
keeping his hero worship to himself,
and the ego-certainty that he would
soon rival the master, sooner than anyone would believe.

Later he saw Joyce again
on the streets of Frankfurt where
they bowed in greeting, said nothing,
politely opened doors for one another, said nothing,
finally separated, one on each side of the street,
walking slowly along the sidewalk,
peering into store windows,
looking at the reflection of the other in the glass.

Joyce amused, perhaps, or bored,
while Wolfe, in unshaken awe,
gauged the reflection of the great writer,
in the shiny windows—the image so small
compared to his own massiveness,
self-absorption, and unfettered verbosity.

The Pyramid Outside Puebla

Planted heavily on the earth,
the pyramid outside Puebla
rose from its thick base to a
sharp point aimed at the heart of god.

Carlos the Iguanero drove the
blue-smoke chugging rattling bus
with his friend Andres up front
who dreamed of driving a truck
in the United States like his uncle Chuy.

They chatted loudly of dreams and Iguanas
but no one really understood and then it was time to be
let out by the small dark entrance where
the archaeologists had dug a narrow trail.

Inside, the path was covered by long sheets of
plywood and open light bulbs were strung
along the sides of the winding walkway to help
guide visitors, dim-eyed and claustrophobic, from
one side of the pyramid to the other.
Deep inside, there were small steps, up and down,
tight corners to maneuver, time to think about the

settling of large rocks and the
odds of an earthquake shaking the stones down and
leaving you buried for eternity among the ruins of
the lost civilizations of Mexico's central valleys.

For longer than most really wanted, the path went on
and on, until the less courageous t
ook quick shallow breaths and
longed for the other side
of the massive monument, hoped to see
light soon and the Mexican sky
and the waiting bus to go back home.

Finally, the pyramid ended and they were back outside,
outside in the sun, with the Mexican sky above and the
Mexican earth below and there was
Carlos the Iguanero and his friend Andres
who dreamed of making a
better living in the north
but would never leave and they were
joking and laughing and jokes were made

about how Carlos got his name and the
tourists were damned glad
to get out of there and later tell people bravely
how they had felt the presence of Mexico's twisting
bloody past while they traversed
the dimly lit trail beneath
the mighty pyramid outside Puebla.

The Old Man

Was on aisle three arguing with a can of pork and beans.
He had on a frayed golfer's cap
covering a really bad toupee,
one of those that never fit, not for a single moment,
and it stuck up wildly from the back
of his scrawny chicken neck.
He yelled at a cantaloupe in fruits and vegetables,
cursed a pound of bacon in meats and cheese,
then charged the paper products
like they were an enemy machine gun nest.
"Same crap for sixty years," he said
as he fought his way through the store
past the nervous stock boys,
up and down the rows of food and drink,
"always the same, nobody ever gets it."
For someone so hostile to groceries
his basket was nearly full
by the time he reached the checkout stand.
On line, he snarled and sniffed at the tabloids,
their covers showing starlets in various stages

of skeletal-like anorexia, and he shook his old head
at the latest visit to earth of equally emaciated space aliens.
The checkout girl rang up his purchases—
never once looking at him—
and she jumped slightly when he howled at a particularly
egregious headline he spotted in the local paper.
"Same old crap," he growled, causing
nearby patrons to whisper among themselves,
"it never changes. Nothin' but garbage."
"I'm sorry sir," the checkout girl said,
"sh..should I call the manager?"
"Sixty years," the old man said, grabbing his groceries
and change from the young girl.
"I'm sorry," she repeated.
The other patrons looked around the store—
at their feet, at the ceiling, off into space.
"You don't get it," the old man growled, "do you?"
Nobody did, of course, nobody but him, the old man.
Jabbering away, he exited the store and
disappeared into the vast parking lot beyond.
The checkout girl rang up her next customer
with a great, relieved smile.
The business of the store went on as usual,
loud, bustling, indifferent.

J.B.
HOGAN

George Bernard Shaw

Rode his bicycle poorly,
wobbly this way, wiggling that
flat into the horse's flanks
in busy Haymarket,
a spidery twist of mangled iron

On to Mrs. Jenny Patterson's flat
or over there to Miss Besant's
the theatre with Florence Farr
into town with a lurch
for sweet Janet Achurch or
sad suicide Eleanor Marx

And down the hill to Tintern Abbey
flailing this way, right and left
towards Mr. Bertrand Russell
a friend-creating, philosopher's crash

Motorcycles and automobiles next,
dapper GBS spinning out and
through the fence to crash
sliding down a long, steep place
finally brakes the car and
stops at last

No harm, save that to
Mrs. Charlotte Payne-Townshend Shaw
herself not quite so Irish lucky
as once she'd been when worth her Salt of Kate
or wearing Alice's Lockett

Lottie being, after all, the
ultimate Nobel Laureate's prize, his life-long love,
save those before and those aft like
charming Mrs. Patrick Campbell and the
luscious, clinging Molly Thompkins

Steady boon companion, Mrs. S.,
setting aside her husband's dalliances,
sexual and political,

here a Mussolini, there a Hitler,
mere mental detours for the
celebrated playwright, the man and not
superman.

End Game

Half century gone in passing
the great divide over-crossed;
all bonus hereinafter coming,
all extra given to surprise.

Choices fewer now but clearer
time shortened, heightened, valued, too;
final age approaching quickly,
the play at end now paramount.

Move by move as chess in flesh
selecting this, releasing that;
all pawns now gone,
kings and bishops moot.

Final steps make up each passing day
last castles guarded, nights colder—dark;
end game personal and private,
played out eternally.

Empire Reborn

Follow the trail, track the path,
go down that road, take the Appian way.
All roads lead back to Rome, and further still
to the city states of Greece.

Track it forward again, follow the path:
Athens to Rome, mighty Rome,
weakened by Cross, overrun by Vandal, terrorized by Hun,
lost for centuries, nearly forgotten in time.

Reborn then in Europe, England, Ireland, too,
spread through church, through ages dark and cold.
Mixed with Norman, Gaul, and Gael,
still onward reaching, still ocean crossing.

At last the new world all roots entwine,
building the next world, the empire reborn.

Eroding Lions

Lion guards framing tall stairs,
outstretched legs inflexible,
ivory-hued haunches marble-frozen, massive.

Protectors of the once great edifice
uprisen beyond visitor's horizon,
wide, vertical, significant.

Now the unused halls reverberate
with rare echoes of unexpected
heels on tile.

Few come now,
few take the time;
all that remains of interest
are the guards, the lions.

Lions bracing the entrance,
rigidly passive, their slow erosion
an observable token
of diminished purpose for that
which lies beyond, behind;
near forgotten moldy stacks—
a treasure poignantly unremembered,
unimaginably to be lost.

Your Little Rabbi

I wanted to like your little rabbi
but you insisted he was something
that he wasn't:
an alien, more than a man.

And those books, those stories:
tales that couldn't happen,
tales that didn't happen.

It was always such a plain story, too,
one that needed no lies,
no embellishment.

A story fine the way it was
needing no rework, no fantasies, no silly myths;
the story of a real man, an honest man of principle.

A man who refused the weakness of his own day,
a man who died unfairly,
killed and reborn falsely,
by the willful ignorance of man.

How White

On the hills of greasy grass
down the coulees to the land
across the river,
where the people waited
to be left alone, waited
for the past to return—
they came.

Hundreds shouting, shooting,
water splashing beneath steel hooves,
smoke rising into the blue sky,
fear rising, men mounting,
the battle joined, led.
Across the river,
up the coulees
to the hills of greasy grass,
they rode to fight, to kill, to win.

In the late day, in the still air,
the women moved among the dead
to cut off their hope for the next world
cleaning their ears so they could hear the people better.

"Oh, see," the old doctor said later, scanning the
cold, bloody field, at the defeated,
at the pieces left there,
at the bodies piled against each other:
"How white they are, how white."

Flashback

Rock and cement chips scattered
on dusty, littered streets, flashback:
bamboo and jungle ferns strewn
on soggy, grass-covered paths.

Wide, arid plains spread out below
distant, gray-brown mountains, flashback:
narrow, rain-gorged rivers leading
to far, foggy, claustrophobic green hills.

Humvee and Bradley tanks; rattling
patrols on death-dealing roads, flashback:
Jeep and ancient APC; rumbling
missions on body-littered streets.

F-16 and Blackhawk helicopters firing
over minaret and into sacred mosque, flashback:
F-4 and Huey helicopters strafing
over temple and into forgotten village.

Desert camo, young and buff
fighting the new millenium's crusade, flashback:
jungle camo, young and on self-destruct
fighting to win the long, cold war.

War of liberation, freedom, and the
imposition of unenforceable democracy, flashback:
war of disengagement, democracy and the
imposition of unenforceable freedom.

$150 Per

Overall, it was not a good month for the fighter wing on temporary duty in South Korea. On the third, two airmen lost control of their jeep, ran off the flight line into a deep ditch and were seriously injured. On the twelfth of the month, two F-4 Phantom jets made back-to-back emergency landings, putting the wing in a skittish mood. Then on the twentieth, ill-tempered Major Peterson, flying without a backseat weapons man, made a sharp turn in a cloud bank and put his F-4 point blank into the side of a mountain.

Authorities conducted the subsequent investigation quietly and quickly, but rumors circulated nonetheless that the accident was neither equipment nor pilot error. Finally, just as things were settling down from the major's death, a young First Lieutenant lost control of his aircraft and dropped it flat down on a small local village.

Early reports were erratic but slowly the real story drifted in. The aircraft developed mechanical trouble some twenty minutes out from base. The pilot and his backseat navigator/weapons man bailed out.

The thick F-4, on its own, flopped crazily, then dropped like a screaming, metallic rock dead into the middle of the village. Many people were home and casualties were high. Twenty-one injured and thirteen dead at final count.

The young lieutenant came into wing headquarters the next morning pasty faced, eyes darting from side to side. Airman Owens, nearing the end of his four-year hitch and the clerk for flight operations commander Lt. Colonel Jackson, watched the lieutenant quietly come into headquarters and timidly pass his desk. The frightened junior officer knocked gently on Colonel Jackson's door. At the sound of the colonel's gruff order to enter, the young lieutenant slipped into the room and gingerly closed the door.

Owens couldn't resist trying to hear what was being said but the sound was muffled by the door. He only heard the colonel's voice rise a couple of times. After twenty minutes or so, the lieutenant emerged. He looked much the same as when he had come in, shaken and scared.

Another in-house investigation followed, quiet and quick as in the case of Major Peterson. When it was over the young pilot was cleared of any culpability in the crash. The Air Force made arrears with the grief-stricken villagers and provided funeral arrangements for the dead. The base chaplain assisted in the emotional memorial services held shortly afterwards.

Even Colonel Jackson attended. He carried official condolences from the U.S. government and checks in the amount of $150 per dead Korean National. The checks went to surviving family members, or in cases where there were none, to a local village fund.

The colonel gave a brief, subdued speech on the strength of Korean-American relations. He reminded the assemblage of all that the two countries had been through together. He stressed their mutual concerns and defense strategies, their long, close association as trading partners, their combined mission to thwart the menace of communism.

A twenty-one gun salute followed the service and everyone went home. The Koreans to their tiny hooches, the GIs back to base.

Afterwards, at wing headquarters, Airman Owens and his two bored communications center buddies, Taglia and Doherty, talked about the incident.

"So what did you guys think of that funeral deal, huh?" Taglia, a burly Connecticut kid with a perpetual five-o'clock shadow, asked.

His partner, Doherty, a short, thin Irish boy from far upper Manhattan shrugged.

"I guess," Owens said, "now we know what a human being is worth."

"At least what a KN is worth," Doherty added pointedly.

"A hundred and fifty bucks," Taglia said.

"A hundred and fifty," Owens repeated. The three young men shook their heads and laughed humorlessly.

After a moment, Owens sighed and walked back into his office. There were bombing practice plans to type up before the end of the day and Colonel Jackson expected them on time.

The crash "incident" was over and there was nothing else to be done or said about it. The mission of the wing would continue as it always had. That was all there was to that. It was really simple stuff.

Dissolving to Nothing

Anachronistic ghosts, the walking dead,
stumble in transition from one age to another,
feverish, weak.

Hoary-bearded, with leaky, bloodshot eyes,
eyes red from having read
the official final verdict,
an inescapable death notice.

Weaving in and out
among the cardboard crowds,
they go unnoticed now—
almost.

And yet, amid the cackling and the crowing,
these ragged hunks of time's refuse still
construct elaborate empty castles
of empty words and dreams—
draw great blueprints in the air
that drift and float, like fading smoke rings,
dissolving to nothing in the vacant, blank sky.

Mushroom Visions

Mushroom visions in black and white,
budding sight,
a triumph of science—
nuclear babies televisionized.

A small woman moans in labor
cities disintegrate,
shadows burn into, onto walls
end one era and out.

Time is come, time is coming,
time is beginning and time has run out for:

Quiet evenings at home,
god myths (slow dying though they are),
a single history,
a simple past,
some unlikely hope.

Theoretically, it is said,
man is yet an adolescent
in the continuum of eternity—
with wet pants
and a hair trigger.

A-Bomb Saturday

"Rolling across the desert," the narrator's voice boomed into the half-filled Royal Theatre, "comes the latest in Yankee ingenuity. Developed secretly, scientists have built a weapon powerful enough to deter any enemy." He paused dramatically and half a hundred hands reached for popcorn, candy, soda.

"Wheeled into position," he went on authoritatively, "it looks like an oversized howitzer. But no, this is the newest cold war weapon, the atomic cannon. With a blast far greater than that which leveled Hiroshima and Nagasaki, this blunderbuss has an effective range unmatched on land."

The Royal audience stared at the flashing screen, transfixed. Forgotten was the laughter of earlier cartoons as well as the "Blackhawks" serial and western feature yet to come.

"In a remote Nevada site," the narrator continued, "a model city was built to show the power of this new, mobile weapon. As soldiers and top brass watch from the safety of concrete bunkers, the order is given. Fire!"

Sending out flickering, shadowy images that reflected on small cheeks and alert eyes, the fireball raged onscreen. Then came the billowing mushroom cloud and fire winds that nearly leveled the mock city. Nearby trees, doubled over by the blazing hurricane, swung back upright, scorched bare.

"There it is," the narrator enthused, "the latest in America's arsenal of war, both a scientific breakthrough and clear deterrent to our enemies."

Between reels, wide eyes blinked in the dark, seats creaked, low talk resumed. Moments later the "Blackhawks" serial began and as the heroes overpowered heinous villains, rumbling cheers began, grew, cascaded triumphantly through the Royal.

Simultaneously, the relieved crowd released a pent up breath of air. With atomic cannons and the Blackhawks, you knew you were plenty safe. No enemy could beat them. You were plenty safe – and that was a darn good feeling.

In His Presence

From side to side he moves,
now forward, then back;
turning, looking toward a middle row,
pointing a sharp-nailed finger in accusation,
determined, preacher-like, combative.

No one breathes, no one moves,
not at this time;
not with another already selected out,
not if there's no reason to,
not when it's not you, not when it's safe.

Angered, he steps down the aisle,
face flushed, ready;
he always wins, he cannot lose,
he will not stop
until the loser, head-bowed, cowed,
word-shattered,
is beaten beyond question
          beyond recognition
          beyond retaliation
here, in this room,
on these aisles,

in his presence.

To Arc Once More

You always knew the latest scandal,
didn't you?
And the local news, sports, weather.
Anything and everything,
to fill up the tedium of your
lost and empty time.

But what about other stuff—
like the Scottsboro Boys,
Red Emma, Phyllis Wheatley,
the goddamn Wobblies for cryin' out loud?

You were thinking
sugar plums, Easter bunnies, and
jolly old St. Nick and missed
the shadows burnt forever on forgotten Japanese walls,
UFC in Guatemala, Alcoa in the DR—
and what about Alger Hiss, for god's sake?

Didn't anyone ever stop to ask,
or even think about,
consider the chance
that someone else might find out?
Didn't it seem to matter?

Was the end result so assured,
the effort so simple, the cost so low,
your arrogant, presumed success so grand
that even now you fail to hear
the whistling of the pendulum,
arcing back, swinging back,
blade sharp and steel hard,
its deep cut into your false history
real and inevitable?

He Was a Big Man

He was a big man to a ten-year old,
tall and strong, with at least
a brace of horses he'd trained
grazing in the L-shaped, fenced field
behind the house we rented.

He had ridden rodeo exhibitions
in the 30s and was so skilled
he made enough money
to escape the hollow where
the slave families, like his parents,
collected down below the town square
after the terrible war between
the governments.

He had a little house just to the south
of his big field, the field I crossed
every day on my way to school
and he kept to himself except in the spring
when he came over and plowed our garden.

I remember watching him,
this tall, dignified man,
walking behind one of his horses,
the small plow digging the dark soil
into deep, straight rows.

He stayed in his little house
until his death, long after we left,
and when I read his obituary
I remembered this tall, straight man,
whose first name we all knew
but never used.

He was Mr. Taylor to us then,
he will always be Mr. Taylor;
adroit horseman, stalwart man,
good neighbor.

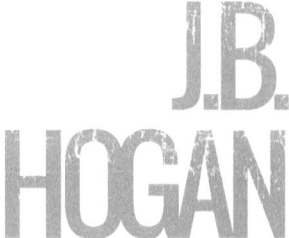

A Little History

Kristallnacht, Sudetenland, Poland 1939,
China, Burma, North Atlantic boats sunk;
Tojo, Hirohito, Admiral Yamamoto, too
Zeros in the blue skies over Diamond Head Bay.

Bataan, Corregidor, Philippines retreat,
London under blackout, children bussed to the north;
Italy, Germany on sandy Egyptian soil
the second front opens, Russia under siege.

Japan in Manila, Singapore, and Rangoon
but Stalingrad holds, Rommel falls at El Alamein;
Allies in Tripoli, Tunis and more
a shift in the wind, a shift in the tide.

Potsdam, Dresden, Yalta, and Berlin
Roosevelt, Stalin, Churchill, et. al.;
Mussolini dead, drug along for a ride
Hitler in his bunker, a necessary suicide.

Then strange clouds fill the New Mexico sky
Big Boy loaded onto the Enola Gay;
surprise and fire in the morning's light,
shadows on walls—a new kind of display.

VE Day, VJ Day, signatures on the Missouri deck,
a broken world left to divide;
western, eastern, Soviet Union, United States,
occupied nations for a half hundred years—
war at last over,
war never to cease.

Just Half Done

Artillery smoke lay atop the valley
in a shifting blue haze;
floating, curling, insinuating itself
into battered ravines, over barren gray soil.

Above the valley,
over rocky contested ridges,
a washed out, cold sun climbed into
a washed out, white sky;
giving no heat to those below,
no promise of warmth to come.

Fear settling over field, like smoke over day
late morning, still air—a whistling sound—
explosion crying, ducking down;
a light, chill wind passed by.

Oaths under cold breath muttered,
prayers to gods unheld;
a call to courage shouted,
the order to fix bayonets.

Up from below, then, in gray waves they came,
wave after wave, unrelenting,
a pause, a prayer again, a hope, another wave;
air snapping metal darts, everywhere whistling.

Whistling toward target, now thundering,
unheard orders up and down the line,
a final lost whisper, a plea for life;
all unheeded in the battle's cold blast.

Point blank firing at the last, last glimpse of light,
quieter now, quieter still, full quiet at last;
hushed moving among khaki bodies,
bayonet probing through cloth and flesh, below bone—
all still.

All still now, all done,
all struggle done, all ceased;
not quite one o'clock yet,
the day just half done.

Kerosene Heat

Heat stoves in the tents were actually five gallon gas cans, the kind usually seen on backs of jeeps. The primer mechanism had to be pumped hard and fast to get the heater started. When they finally caught on they were just as hard to keep going. They always went out the first night or two until the primer automatically fed fuel to the fire.

Each ten-man tent had one of these heaters and the men loosely alternated responsibility for keeping the fire going. It got very cold at night in a tent in Korea and until the stove was primed good, every time it went out the tent was like a morgue—freezing cold.

On the first night they moved the enlisted men in Owens' outfit into the Corps of Engineers hastily erected area immediately named tent city, the heater in Owens' tent went out. It had been a hassle all night. They primed and re-primed it until around ten-thirty it began putting out heat fairly well. The men jumped into their cots and pulled the covers tight against their bodies. They hoped the can would stay lit all night. It didn't.

Owens woke about four-thirty a.m., so cold his nose felt like it had been stuck in an iceberg. He was afraid to move, the blankets and sheets so icy he feared the chilling effect of even the slightest accidental contact with them. He lay perfectly still for at least ten or fifteen minutes, heard some of the other men stirring, waited for somebody else to get up and start the fire. Nobody did. After another ten minutes he heard a whispering sound from the cot behind him.

"Hsst, hsst," came the low sound. It was Upshaw. "Hsst, hsst."

"What do you want, Upshaw?"

"Somebody gotta start the fire."

"Yeah," Owens agreed. A bed across the tent creaked.

"The hawk done come right on in here on us, man."

"I'm hip."

"Is it almost morning?"

"No way."

"Man, that fire gotta get going."

"You gonna do it?"

"I ain't getting up, brother," Upshaw said. "It's too cold."

It got quiet again and Owens heard Upshaw roll over in his bunk. Just the sound of the movement made Owens shiver. He tried to go back to sleep himself. He couldn't. He lay there, each minute ticking off like an hour, listening to the low breathing of his tent mates. He realized no one else was going to get up.

Mustering every bit of resolve he could find in his unwilling spirit, Owens forced himself out of bed. With a shudder, he drug his legs across the white tundra of the sheets, pushed back the blanket, and swung his feet towards the floor. His toes barely touched the rigid wood before he dashed them into the slightly less chilling tops of his boots and down into the heavy socks buried within. Sitting upright, feet angled into his boots, arms tight at his sides, Owens, in his white long john shirt and pants, was an immobile apparition in the otherwise blackness of the tent.

He sat that way for several moments, colder than he'd ever been in his life. He realized that donning his fatigue uniform would, at least initially, be unimaginably colder. He felt for the pants and found them and his fatigue shirt beside the boots. He knew it was really stupid not to have put those fatigues inside the bed with him. They would be warm now, instead of feeling like some sadistic dry cleaner had starched them with dry ice. He managed an unseen, sardonic smile.

With a rush he put on his socks, pulled his pants up with a deep breath, and practically leapt into his boots. He stood up then, breathed quickly, waited for his body to warm up the shoes, socks and pants. He dreaded putting on the shirt. But he did, and then the field jacket and baseball cap. He was completely dressed, bootlaces untied. Bending to tie those just now, he reasoned, was taking the whole thing too far. He unhooked the kerosene can from the stove and shuffled off for the door.

Outside it was impossibly, ridiculously cold. He set the can down and reluctantly tied his bootlaces halfway up. When he stood straight again he realized his jaw and lower lip were jutting out like an ugly bull dog or a film clip he'd once seen of Winston Churchill puffing on a stogie. He relaxed his face muscles and walked to the end of the tent row. Several big kerosene tanks had been mounted on wooden platforms there.

Positioning the can on a ledge beneath the spigot on one of the tanks, Owens released a slow flow of kerosene into the five gallon drum. As he peered into the darkness to make out the movement of the kerosene from tank to can, Owens realized he was finally awake. He wasn't as cold as he had been before in the tent, but he was aware that it was incredibly cold. He actually sort of felt good. Nobody else had got up to get the kerosene. He breathed in deeply, feeling the crisp air in his nostrils and lungs. He took a moment to look around.

Across the paved road to his left and up a couple of hundred yards, he distinguished the outline of the base gym where they were taking their showers until the Corps of Engineers got a shower tent built. Sighting above the objects he wanted to see at night – as he had been taught as a child and reinforced in the service – Owens identified the base chapel and vaguely made out an officer's hut in the darkness beyond. Everywhere else was tents, row after row, sitting like frozen frogs on the dead Korean soil.

As he stood there in the dark cold, Owens recalled another bone chilling moment just a few days before when his outfit had been called out to tear rotten, useless tents from their icy, obsolete dumpster homes. It made him think of the men who had fought the war, now so long ago. It must have been horribly cold in the foxholes. Owens was sure he could have never done it. He couldn't even have stood the cold, much less fought in it. Just imagining such a thing gave him another shiver. He opened the kerosene tank spigot another notch.

Except for the sound of the kerosene running, it was virtually still on the base. Owens looked up at the sky for the first time and saw that it was perfectly clear. The stars twinkled briskly and the Milky Way made a broad white swath across the night sky just as he'd known it as a kid.

In the quiet cold, with the awesome sky above, Owens felt small, insignificant, alone. At first the thought frightened him, made him feel colder. But then the fear lifted, and he felt a mild rush of internal warmth.

He smiled at the distant stars. Things weren't so bad after all. A guy could still feel okay. Even in a place like this, even in a winter like this. Blowing frosty air out of his mouth, Owens topped off the can of kerosene and walked calmly, if quickly, back to the tent.

Inside, he cranked up the stove, primed it over and over until it caught, held, put out heat. He stood right on top of the stove until it was going good, until the chill was gone from his clothes, his bones. Eventually, when he was warm enough, he sat back down on the edge of his cot. He did not go back to sleep.

By the time the tent was mostly warm, the rest of the men began to stir. They chattered loud enough to wake Upshaw, who stretched and rolled over in his cot towards the stove. Owens looked at his friend who peeked one eye from behind the covers.

"Come on up out of there, Lonnie," he laughed. "It's surfin' weather, dude."

"Surfin', my eye," Upshaw pushed back the covers and yawned broadly, "ain't no brothers do no surfin' in no Korea, man." Owens laughed again.

"Brother, the hawk was flat out last night. You got the kerosene and this thing goin'?"

"I did."

"It must've been mighty cold out there, huh?"

"It was cold enough." Owens looked down at his shoes. He felt pretty good about getting the place warmed up for his buddies. "At least the wind wasn't blowin'."

"Well, you done good," Upshaw said, buttoning the top of his fatigue pants and gingerly slipping his olive drab shirt on over his long-handle top. "You done fine."

At ease then, Owens laid down on his cot, stared at the green canvas roof until the rest of the guys headed out to the chow hall for breakfast. He rested in the warm air, smiling to himself. After a quarter of an hour or so, he finished tying his brogans and headed off to the chow hall, too. It was a cold, clear, bright winter day. Pretty much standard for Korea.

His buddies were already clearing out when Owens got to the mess hall, so he sat at an empty table in a corner of the room. He felt pretty good, relaxed, content. He ate a big meal and went back for seconds. Not even powdered eggs and SOS, the mysterious chipped beef in gravy on toast concoction known to all servicemen for all time, could mar his mood this morning.

Later he would stop by the base exchange and get some potato chips or candy bars for snacking in the tent, if they had any. Maybe tonight the fire would stay on all the way till morning. Or somebody else would get up in the dark and cold and keep it going. Owens had done his part for the time being. He felt pretty good about that.

He Was Fallen

He was fallen,
but not like Joyce:
about to fall but not yet fallen.
No, he had really fallen—
hard, unchecked, for a decade or more.

It wasn't your average fall, or
a metaphorical descent into hell.
It was a real fall—
a knuckle-bustin', continuous tumble down
as far as he could fall fall.

It could have been worse:
he could have been tortured or maimed,
he could have died.

He definitely could have used some help,
he could have used a break,
could have used some R & R.

In the end he was lucky to have survived—
if that's what you call it—lying there at the
bottom of a decade with no way out and the
top of time so far away and untouchable.

Through the Years

Gaunt, white-haired man,
father to children unborn.
Weak, feverish, failing man,
teller of tall tales, generations' center.

Aged, white-haired man,
towering snow-topped mountain.
Chiseled from eighty years,
of eroding earth and dream.

Tired, white-haired man,
anachronism of a passing age.
Enfeebled, unsure, dying man,
yet provider still of strength, of family pride.

Ancient, white-haired man,
sufferer of a final terrible, false doubt.
The sound of rifle shot into that last, cold night;
still echoing down these long, these many years.

Looking Back

Looking back isn't always the best thing to do,
it's wiser to just keep your
      shoulder into the wind
      nose to the grindstone
      eyes on the road
      hands on the wheel,
that's the better idea, the far better plan.

Looking back can be a little unsettling,
it might cause you to realize that you
      weren't very brave very often
      didn't treat others like you should have
      didn't accomplish much with your life
      failed to live up to expectations,
      yours or anyone else's;
not good things to remember, to recall too clearly,
not this late.

No, looking back isn't always the best thing,
it might best be avoided, unless you want to
      recall
      remember
      feel
      know...
no, looking back is definitely not good,
it's not good at all.

An Old Dream

He felt uneasy, out of place. He thought it was China; it might have been Burma. But he was there, wherever it was. He stood on the sun deck of a multi-level wood home that jutted precariously from a rich, deep, green, tropical hillside. Near him were several Asians about whom he knew little. One of them was a pretty young woman with shiny black hair falling magnificently from under her inverted funnel hat and halfway down her back.

He and the others watched the far horizon. Carefully. Waiting for something. What that something was, was not clear. For a long time he panned the distant hills and forests. Waiting. Watching. For what? For something, he was sure. All the while nothing was said. Nothing heard. It was as if the world were mute or he was deaf. Then came the dread.

He knew something terrible was about to happen. It was what he had been looking for. Something awful was going to happen there—at the horizon, at the edge of the green forest below and beyond them. He felt nauseated and things began slowing down. The people near him stirred slightly, gradually. There was still no sound.

Then came a flash of light. Not as bright as he expected. But he knew it was what he'd been waiting for. He knew he'd known all along. Far off it rose. Boiling, spinning, climbing in an expanding column. A vast structure of wind, heat, and cloud. It billowed up in the distance, nearly assuming its final, awesome shape before the first wind rustled through the trees.

Almost at the horizon, at the base of the fully developed cloud, there was a subtle, swaying in the trees. It was like the inner ripple in a circle of water created by a stone tossed into a pond or still creek. It slowly moved towards him and the others. All of them stood motionless, stunned by the overwhelming spectacle.

He thought of his family and friends, of those beside him, and he felt a kind of hopeless resignation. A kind of emotionless emotion or perhaps an emotion denied its outpouring by the obvious futility of its expression. He knew there was nothing he could do about anything. He couldn't even wish to do anything because nothing could be done. It was all over.

He felt the wind in stages. Lightly at first, then stronger. Then the heat. And the deck began to shake and sway. It pitched to the side and broke from its foundations. Oddly, he made no effort to move even when the floor fell out from beneath and he and the others fell towards the lush jungle floor below. As they dropped there was a last, furious wave of heat and *wind and he noted how inevitable it all was – how self-fulfilling, so outside the control of anyone or anything. And then it was really over.*

—

He couldn't believe it, but the shaking began anew. Persistent, annoying. He found he could move again. He found his voice.

"What?" he fought to open his eyes. "What?"

"Hey," a voice called, "wake up."

"Huh?"

"I said, wake up."

He rolled over on his back and looked up.

"Jesus Christ," Strader hovered over him, "you were groaning like mad. Wake up."

"I'm awake now," he rubbed his eyes. Strader walked across the room and sat down on his own bed.

"Jeez, I must have been dreaming."

"Must have been a hell of a dream," Strader said.

"I guess so."

"You remember it?"

"No, just vague stuff. Something weird with green country and Chinese or something."

"Green Chinese?" Strader laughed.

"No."

"It was a joke," Strader pulled on his boots.

"Oh."

"Must have been a hell of a dream." Strader repeated.

"Yeah."

"You were sure groanin' like crazy."

"Yeah?"

"Yep."

"I think I've had that dream before. I have a feeling I have."

"I'll pass on it myself," Strader stood up. "I'll let you have it." They both laughed.

"Thanks."

"No sweat. Green Chinese."

"I'm sure I've had it before."

"Probably have. A lot of people have the same dream. Over and over."

"That's probably it," he nodded. "It seems familiar even though I can't remember the details. You know what I mean?"

"Sure, but it's over now. You might as well forget it. Dreams aren't real."

"They sure seem like it sometimes."

"It's a game your mind plays."

"I guess so."

"Yeah, that's it."

"Well, I'm awake now. That's the reality."

"What's so great about reality?"

"It's better than that dream."

"You goin' to chow?"

"Yeah," he said. "I'll be there in a minute."

"Better hurry or all the good stuff'll be gone," Strader kidded.

"Right," he said dully, "whatever."

"Whatever."

When Strader was gone, he finished putting on his uniform and boots, locked up his closet, and headed to the chow hall. Outside, he was surprised to see how late in the day it was.

I hate swing shifts, he told himself, looking at the distant mountains beyond the site. The terrain looked nothing like that in the dream. That was a good thing, but the feel of the dream was hard to shake. You never have any free time on swings, you're always tired.

That's probably why I had that damn dream, he thought, feeling profoundly alone as he entered the semi-crowded chow hall. Lots of people probably have dreams like that, especially when they are tired. And swings really made you tired. Tired and lonely feeling. Susceptible to dumb dreams. And feeling lonely.

He stood in the serving line until he realized they were dishing out roast beef. The last time they'd served the thin-sliced meat he had gingerly turned it over with his fork and found a rainbow sheen on the underside. Replacing his tray, he decided he'd eat something else, someplace else. That roast beef was unacceptable.

With his head still mostly in a cloud, he walked out of the chow hall—not seeing Strader's arm-flailing attempt to get his attention—and headed toward the gig, the work compound.

"I hate swing shifts," he muttered as he walked along, half-expecting his dream to suddenly manifest itself in reality.

The sun, setting behind the mountains far in the distance to his left, lit the buildings and roads around him in a weak, yellowish light. Sighing deeply, he lowered his head and, concentrating on the shiny tops of his boots, tramped on to work.

Guardabarranco

Schoolroom hot from the afternoon
Nicaraguan sun, stuffy, humid,
lessons imperfectly learned, new
friends not quite found, then a
door opened, they walked in—
he tall and solid, guitar in hand,
she lithe, lovely with angel's voice,
students gathered round, before, sat,
listened to gleaming stories,
shimmering mixture of instrument and
sweet vocal filling the
close air with beauty and power of
dream, a dream edging toward a reality
complex, fragile, hoping to live on
against harsh odds under the hot
Nicaraguan sun.

Gabriel Heatter Mornings

Awaken to Gabriel Heatter mornings,
stirring to the smell of eggs, bacon,
skillet toast fried with shortening, the
milkman bringing small bottles of
chocolate milk with paper lids.

Inside a child's world
there were few distractions—
no McCarthyism befouling the air,
no concern for Hiss entering the unformed brain.

Just a warm place for a child, free from:
"Give 'em hell, Harry,"
MacArthur's last return,
mangled bodies in Eastern fields.

Watching the others go to school,
tears staining front door windows,
the ultimate pain, their return the ultimate joy.

At night to bed beneath electric suns;
that could be turned on or off,
then dreams of eggs, bacon,
skillet toast fried with shortening, the
milkman leaving small bottles of
chocolate milk with paper lids.

Six Blocks from the *Zocalo*

It was about six blocks
from the zocalo in Mexico City
lurking silently on a corner
like some gravity-crushing
gray stone monolith—
which it was.

From without, it said nothing much about
a god or son or any organized rites.
Thousands passed by it each day,
taking no notice at all.

But it was very hot outside,
bright yellow sunny, and
inside, in the interior, it
surely would be dark and cool.

And it was.

And it wasn't spectacular,
not like the Catedral Metropolitano,
but it had a surprising charm,
its icons, its wooden pews,
its bulletin board with the many
milagros of the faithful pinned there.

It was a quiet place, after all,
a refuge from the heat, the sound, the people and,
back outside, an unnoticed shade tree
under which one could rest a moment,
readjust to the weather, take a deep breath,
then plunge back into the day,
back into the sweltering crowds,
back into the heart of the great city,
the vibrant, acrid center of Mexico itself.

La Mordida

AeroNica Flight 242 from Managua touched down without incident at the Mexico City Airport just after noon on a bright, sunny fall day. Kyle Alexander and Wendy Bennet, back from a church-sponsored, three-week fact finding mission to Nicaragua, had earlier only passed through the Mexican capitol on their way to Central America. Now, with a couple of free days before they had to return to their separate Wisconsin hometowns, the new friends planned to spend some time seeing the sights of Mexico City.

"I heard they have a storage area here in the airport," Wendy pulled a suitcase behind while she carried a thick pack on her back as well. Kyle had a stuffed pack on his back, too, and was carrying a cloth bag of mail he'd been asked to deliver to the states by the many international workers they'd met in Managua. "Maybe we can put some of this stuff up until we leave."

"Good idea," Kyle agreed.

Towards one end of the airport, they found a storage

area and a lady on duty stored their heavier and more awkward belongings. She gave them a ticket for later pick up. They bought a taxi ticket at a nearby exit and rode into the *Zocalo*, or town center, of the huge city.

"I heard about a quiet hotel a couple of blocks from here," Wendy said, as they backpacked from near the metropolitan cathedral.

The Hotel Francisco was as Wendy advertised, quiet— and perhaps more importantly, inexpensive. The rooms were clean, if sparsely furnished, the only drawback being a shortage of hot water for showers.

After resting briefly, the friends walked back to the *Zocalo* and bought cheap tortas de queso, cheese sandwiches, at one of the many inexpensive taquerías lining the nearby streets. While they ate, Kyle noticed what seemed like a peculiar occurrence outside the front window.

A street corner policeman had cornered a nicely dressed older man and the two seemed to be arguing about something. Both men vigorously made their points, waved their arms excitedly. Finally, Kyle saw the older man reach into his pockets and hand something, perhaps paper money, to the policeman.

Kyle turned to tell Wendy about the incident when he noticed one of the sandwich makers in the restaurant looking at him.

"*La mordida,*" the worker said to Kyle.

"*La ...que?*" Kyle quizzed, his Spanish not the greatest, though somewhat better than Wendy's.

"*La mordida,*" the man behind the counter repeated.

"En inglés, the bite. This is our way. Mexico, como se dice, economía."

"Mexican economy," Kyle hazarded a guess.

"Así es," the man said.

"Oh," Kyle smiled like he really understood.

"What is he saying?" Wendy looked up from her torta.

"Not one hundred percent sure. Just saw an odd thing outside a minute ago. No big deal.

"Fine with me. This sure is a good sandwich."

"Yeah, mine, too."

After the poverty in Nicaragua, everything in Mexico, including simple cheese sandwiches, seemed downright luxurious.

—

With two days of sightseeing and trinket buying in the open air *mercados*—or markets—around the *Zocalo* behind them, Wendy and Kyle caught a taxi at the Hotel Francisco for the return trip to the airport. At the baggage area where they left their things, they encountered two uniformed guards instead of the lady who helped them before. One guard was seated at a small table, the other stood beside him. They looked friendly enough. Just regular guys in uniform.

"Buenos días," Kyle offered the storage ticket.

"Buenos días, señor," the guard at the table, the younger-looking of the two, took the ticket and looked it over carefully but said nothing else.

"Uh... *nuestras maletas estan alla,*" Kyle said in his best Spanish, pointing towards the storage area. He hoped the guards understood. "Our bags are back there."

The older guard replied but neither understood.

"What's wrong?" Wendy asked.

"I'm not sure. They don't seem to be in any hurry to get our bags."

"We've got to get them. Our flight leaves this morning."

Kyle tried again but the guards still acted like they didn't understand. He could not catch what they were saying, although they seemed to find the situation a little funny.

Slowly, Kyle caught on. The nuances of the situation sank in. The guards, like the policeman outside the *taquería* back by the *Zocalo*, were simply looking for a little something extra to get the things out of storage. Probably nothing too big. Just a tip.

"Oh," Kyle reached into his pockets for a few peso bills and into the depths of his Spanish for the right words, "*un regalito para café?* A little gift for coffee?"

The guards nodded and took the offered money. They immediately retrieved the stored items.

"What happened there?" Wendy asked, as they hustled to catch their flight.

"That was *la mordida,*" Kyle said, "the bite. Like the other night at that *taquería.*"

"Hmm. I'm glad you understand. I would've never known what they wanted."

"I don't know how I did either," Kyle admitted, "but it worked."

"Well, thank you," Wendy smiled, "you really got us out of a spot back there."

"We better hurry up and catch our plane." Kyle tried to act like what had happened with "la mordida" was something a guy like him dealt with on a day-to-day basis. "Don't want to miss it and worry the folks back home."

"No, we wouldn't," Wendy agreed as they hustled on, "we wouldn't want to do that at all."

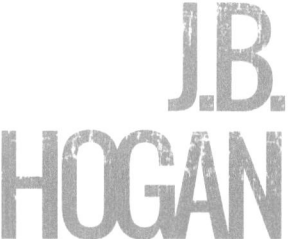

Middle Ground

There is no middle ground—
not anymore.
No more fence straddling;
climb down, pick a side,
stop hiding in that false center.
You're either for it or against it,
make up your mind,
show some guts, show some spine,
stop pretending that it doesn't matter,
that it will be okay.
Be an adult, be yourself.
Stop acting like you don't care,
stop acting like it's all the same;
it's not all the same.
It's for them or against them,
love it or leave it,
one way or the other,
their way or the highway,
put up or shut up.
There's not enough time left now,

you can't just ride along,
balanced on the handlebars anymore.
Give it up, get in the game,
pick a side;
have some heart, show some guts,
be somebody.

I Get That a Lot

He was sitting in a padded lawn chair on the patio
trying to read Gorky Park while
several colorful parrots sporadically squawked
their appreciation of the tropical afternoon.

The three-day fever had broken earlier in the day
and now, as he waited for the fog in his head to clear,
there was a bustling nearby, new arrivals
at the Casa Internaciónal.

He looked over at the noise,
trying to focus his tired, red eyes, and
suddenly she was there, hurrying toward
one of the rooms across the way.

He had never seen, feverish or not,
a woman so beautiful.
Who was she? Why was she here?

He imagined, from her olive-skin
and fine features, that she was an actress—
an actress from some fortunate acting company
from Spain here to perform at the National Theatre.

She came back out of her room again,
saw him, favored him with a radiant smile.
He was sure of it now—a Spanish actress.

Two days later, the fever and fog completely gone,
she introduced herself. From Israel, she said,
just a hydrologist helping the nation produce clean water.
Had never acted, she explained, never even been to Spain.

I knew that, he lied with a weak laugh,
I could tell right away you were an Internacionalista.
It was the fever had me confused, and
the way you look.

She lightly rested her hand on his arm,
presented him a near fatal smile,
of course, she said, it's a natural mix up,

especially down here, I get that a lot.
Of course, he said feebly, of course you do.

Rainmaker

Rainmaker—
word philanthropist,
servant of muses,
guardian of Castalian spring.

Chronicler of youth and age
of Jungian dualities and medieval spirits.

Mellow gardener of Montagnola,
instructor in the terror of love,
show again how to immerse
in the cold lake of selflessness
for the initiates unknown and unseen,
those not yet born,
those who must, those who cannot help
but follow.

Once in a Lifetime

This is how it went down. There were four of us driving around town looking for local girls. It was a little North Carolina town and the odds of us being successful in our quest were pretty poor. That didn't deter us, of course. No call, no sale, was what we used to say.

With our designated driver unhappily remaining sober, we hit a couple of bars to give ourselves some liquid courage in the search for what we thought passed for reasonable social interaction.

Unfortunately, we hadn't been cruising the streets for much over a half hour when our evening plans ran into a snag. It was a carload of local boys and they did not appreciate us roaming up and down their streets looking for their girls.

"Go the hell back where you come from," one of our genial Carolina hosts called out from the front rider's seat of a ratty, twenty-year old Chevrolet sedan.

He punctuated his greeting with several internationally recognized hand signals—which we returned in the spirit of fraternity with which they had been presented.

"Piss off," our sober driver smiled to the Carolinians.

"Pull into the Quickie Mart," the front rider challenged, using that clichéd hand signal again. Some of us were beginning to become perturbed by our inhospitable welcome.

"See you there, Bird Boy," I called out from my back left seat. Bird Boy lifted a middle digit once again. Very little creativity.

The locals zoomed ahead of us and shot into the Quickie Mart parking lot, screeching to a crisp halt in an empty parking space. We pulled in slower and parked right beside them to their left. For a few moments we continued to exchange pleasantries, frequently punctuated by that oh so trite extension of the middle finger. We passed around beer and whiskey to prime ourselves and we could see them doing the same.

"You punks go back to whatever rock you crawled out from under," Bird Boy remarked rudely, jabbing a beer bottle in our direction.

"Good one, Bird Boy," I yelled back. "You're a real bright boy." I liked that line, I had stolen it from a story I'd been reading lately. It seem apropos at the moment.

"I'll give you bright boy," Bird Boy countered. He seemed irrationally aggressive and hostile—perhaps in need of an attitude adjustment.

"You need an attitude adjustment," I told him. My pals laughed. It was a pretty good line.

"Maybe you want to try and do the adjusting," Bird Boy said, pointing his beer bottle at me. "Must be a big war hero or something." His buddies laughed. It was a pretty annoying line.

"Screw you," I said, handing a pint of whiskey to one of my buds.

I opened my door and stumbled out onto the Quickie Mart lot. The lights in the store and by the gas pumps and on the posts around the parking lot seemed very bright with glistening yellow trails coming off of them. I put my left hand against the side of our car and took a deep breath. Then I headed for the other car—on Bird Boy's side.

I had to work a little not to bump into the back end of their car as I headed for an assumed confrontation with these pesky locals. I had not adequately considered what I was going to do when I got face to face with my new antagonist, or his friends, but I was determined to push on with all possible dispatch. Just as I reached the rider's side door, my resolve to adjust Bird Boy's attitude took an unexpected turn.

Bird Boy, anticipating my arrival, swung open his door and put the barrel of a short, small caliber pistol directly into my beer and whiskey expanded stomach. Hmm. I had not considered this possibility. No, this was a new one on me. I wondered briefly what to do. The answer came to me easily, almost instinctively I think, especially considering the circumstances.

With a calmness I had no idea that I would have in such a situation, I stopped pretty much dead in my tracks and then casually folded my arms across my chest. First step —good move. The barrel of that pistol was right against my less than six-pack abs. What next? Leave. That was a good idea.

With arms still crossed, I began backing up, walking slowly, one step at a time, left, then right, then repeat, carefully distancing myself from the pistol in Bird Boy's hand. I kept going backwards until I cleared the back of the locals' car and then I turned and walked at a more determined and faster pace back to our car. Back to my buddies, back to where the pistol that had been aimed at my stomach was a recent memory rather than a current moment of reality.

"That mother has a gun," I pronounced loudly to my pals as I piled back into the car. The brief experience had done wonders for my previous state of inebriation. "He put that sucker right in my guts."

"Let's get out of here," the guy next to me in the back seat declared.

"Hell, yes," our sober designated driver concurred.

He jabbed the car in gear and backed out of the parking space with a big loop that kept us on the left side of our antagonists' car. They suddenly backed out in exactly the same manner, except their big loop put them a few feet behind us. While our driver tried to find a forward gear, the rest of us watched as the locals—who seemed to be scrambling around inside their vehicle—hit the gas and pulled alongside. Just as they got parallel to our car, Bird Boy, now in the back seat behind the driver, leaned out of the window and pointed his pistol right at us.

"Holy crap," the guy beside me hollered, "he's gonna shoot us."

Without warning, the locals' vehicle sped up – I remember hearing our car revving wildly as if the driver was hammering the gas with the transmission in neutral. Bird Boy stuck his pistol out the window and fired at us point blank.

"Jesus," I dove for the back floorboard.

"He's shooting us," the guy beside me yelled.

Crack, came the report of the pistol, followed by an immediate thudding, slapping sound against the side of our car. I buried myself deeper into the floorboard. Crack, came round two. Then the instant thud and slap against the side of the car. A loud squealing of tires was our clue that the locals had gunned their car and were headed out of the parking lot.

I popped up in the back seat, a little dazed and confused. I looked over at the guy beside me. The driver and the guy riding shotgun turned around to look at us. We couldn't believe what had just happened.

"Blanks," somebody said, "he was firing blanks. He had blanks in that pistol."

It took a moment for that information to sink in. The sound had been so real, the slapping against the side of the car so strong it seemed only real bullets could have made such a noise, but they hadn't. The guy beside me looked out the window. There was no damage to the side of the car. No holes.

"Man, I thought we were goners," our driver said. "I thought that was the real thing."

"Let's get those punks," the guy beside me suggested.

"Good idea," the guy riding shotgun agreed.

"I don't know," I shook my head. "That was pretty wild."

"We'll look for 'em," the driver said.

It took about ten or fifteen minutes to locate Bird Boy and his crew but we finally saw them turn at a stoplight and head out of town on a two-lane blacktop road. Our driver put the juice to it and we chased them for a couple of miles until they stopped along the side of the road.

We pulled up on their left again a few feet behind. Our driver angled our car where we were sort of looking at their driver and Bird Boy, who was still in the back left rider's side.

"You ain't got nothin' but blanks in that gun," our driver called out. "You're punks. I ought to come over there and kick your butts."

Bird Boy held up the pistol for everyone to see. He pulled the hammer back to half-cock and spun the cylinder for dramatic effect.

"How do you dumb asses know I didn't switch to live ammo while you were chasing us?" He held up a box of what looked like regular ammunition. "The real McCoy. Feel like running the risk? Or maybe you should turn around and go back into town. Maybe even stay away from town for a while."

"We ain't afraid of you," our driver said.

"Not the point," Bird Boy replied with a twisted smile. "Just a suggestion is all. You can come ahead or go on. But you'll have to see if I'm lyin' or not. Are you up to it?"

We looked at each other again. By this time I figured

we were all as stone sober as our designated driver. There wasn't much we could do about this particular scene. The guy had us buffaloed with that pistol. None of us was willing to gamble on whether the rounds in it now were real or not. The whole situation was a loss, or at best some kind of unsatisfying draw.

"Let's get out of here," I sighed. "These guys are nothin' but local yokel jerks. To hell with them."

We slowly backed away from their car. Bird Boy waived a friendly goodbye with his pistol. We gave him a particular wave of our own and then drove on back into town. Locals 1, Outsiders 0.

For all the excitement of that little episode, it didn't stop us from coming into town looking to have fun. In fact, for the rest of the time we were in that little town we never saw Bird Boy or his pals again. Hell, they may have been from some other little town themselves, just acting like big shots in this one.

Whatever it was, for me it turned out to be a once in a lifetime encounter—a pistol being stuck into my stomach I mean. Sometimes later I would hear people talking about having guns pulled on them and such and talking big about it as if it was something that happened all the time.

If I talk about my experience to anyone, I sure don't talk big about it. No, one time is enough when it comes to having a gun pulled on you and leveled at your guts. Anything more than that begins to sound like Hollywood crap—phony and overdone. In my experience, one time is plenty. It's enough to last a lifetime.

Faulkner in Paris

Faulkner went to Paris in the summer
but nobody noticed.
He grew a beard, smoked a pipe,
adopted Bohemian airs.

No one saw him and he was too shy
to hang with the Beach crowd
or speak to James Joyce and
he sure as hell wasn't going to
hang out with Ernest and his mob.

So while the other expatriates
were mincing before Gertrude's throne,
Bill lived incognito, avoided the crowds,
absorbed the Parisian scene.

In December, he went home
to Mississippi, reanimated,
on fire with literary zeal,
prolifically energized and prepared
to seal his place in literature
for all time to come.

When You Died

When you died
there was only the image of
your lifeless body
in the open bitter coffin—
your hands limp and useless
face not quite real,
jaw too square, the flesh too loose;
your intelligent eyes were closed,
your brilliant mind lost to us,
your voice still, then, forever.

Cadillac Mountain

Winding gently, the shadowed trail
slowly and easily climbed
through spruce and pine
towards wide fields of granite
above and beyond.

Dark and musty, then
out into brilliant light,
shining on grass and rock,
the climb steeper now,
the way direct and clear.

On an outcropping, a pause,
bright flashes of sunlight on sea,
the ocean, blue and unbounded,
stretching to the horizon,
a time to reflect.

Reflections of loss,
of recent passing
in the distant west,
a need for goodbye.

Then farewell at last,
with the immense sea spread
in front, beyond,
below this empty space,
shimmering sunlight reflecting
off the calm sea—the ocean—
the ocean vast and silent,
fathomless, beautiful, placidly aloof.

Sea Plane

It was a typical Caribbean day, bright and sunny. Small puffy cumulus clouds dotted the sky, drifted rapidly by. Small vessels and larger ferry boats cruised back and forth in the busy harbor bouncing on the sparkling, white-capped waters.

The ferries chugged across the harbor packed with passengers on their way to work or play. The small boats moved faster, but with less direct intent, giving their passengers time to admire the shimmering scenery of Old San Juan or the shining Atlantic waters beyond.

Nearer Old San Juan, a sea plane rolled and bobbed in the churning waters. On board the white, new El Caribe Airlines pontooned-craft, besides pilot and co-pilot, were six travelers bound for St. Thomas in the U. S. Virgin Islands.

Among them a middle-aged Canadian couple, happy-faced tourists anticipating the day trip to Charlotte Amalie with its duty-free stores filled with island trinkets and inexpensive alcohol and tobacco products.

Behind the Canadians, a well-dressed, red-faced

man from San Juan, a businessman perhaps or minor government official. Just back of him an old mulatta woman held a smiling, happy little boy who cooed happily.

A quiet sailor sat at the back of the plane, on day leave, perhaps, and looking forward to the excitement of the afternoon bar scene on St. Thomas.

The pilot revved up the immaculate, powerful engines per preflight procedure. The motors hummed smoothly and the passengers watched as onshore crewmen unhooked and retrieved the ropes holding the aircraft to its deplaning dock.

Un-tethered then, the plane drifted and bounced in the rolling waters. Slowly, the pilot taxied the aircraft away from the dock and across the mildly choppy bay towards the sea. With its engines whining towards takeoff speed, the plane moved quickly across the harbor.

The passengers watched out the windows as the plane bounced along going faster and faster. With each passing moment it strove to become more aerodynamic, less ocean-bound. In moments, it barely touched the surface of the bay as the pilot steered it towards open water.

"Oh, how exciting," the Canadian woman enthused, as the plane rattled and shook in its effort to become airborne.

"Wonderful," her husband patted her on the hand.

The well-dressed, red-faced man leaned back in his seat and closed his eyes. The mulatta lady held onto her little charge, who whimpered at the sound of the roaring engines and rough thuds of the pontoons as they fought through the waves. In back, the sailor sat calmly, his face an impassive mask.

Then, just as the plane reached take off speed and the pilot pulled back hard on the yoke to bring it up off the water, an unexpectedly strong wave, the wake from a large ocean-going yacht perhaps, swamped the right pontoon.

The awkward looking plane dipped to starboard, spun up, and rolled over once. Its engines screaming uselessly, the craft crashed flat on its back into the harbor. From a distance it had the look of a large, metallic insect caught in some watery trap. Remarkably, it stayed afloat upside down for several minutes, the slowly sank below the surface.

Fortunately, a nearby Coast Guard rescue boat quickly responded. As the groaning, creaking plane dipped below the surface of the water, Guardsmen threw themselves into the bay and rapidly forced open evacuation doors along the sides of the wrecked aircraft.

In a matter of minutes, the Guard plucked seven people from the wreck, including the dazed pilot and co-pilot. The plane sank too fast for a final rescue run and an eighth person went down with the craft.

Later, when waves in the harbor settled down, Guard divers located the airplane at the bottom of the harbor. When they recovered the last body it was still strapped in a seat at the back of the plane, a half-inch bolt from the cracked fuselage driven neatly into the skull just above the right temple.

The young sailor was brought up carefully and the Guardsmen gingerly laid his body to rest on the harbor dock. One of the rescuers turned the head so that the wound did not show. Before the body was removed, a reporter snapped a photograph but when it appeared in the paper the next day, the young man looked more like a sailor sleeping one off than a corpse.

The following week, a brief funeral service was held at the sailor's San Juan base before the body was shipped for burial to his Midwestern, land-locked hometown. The Navy listed the death as accidental, non-service related. His buddies threw a wake for him and drank several toasts in his honor. For a few weeks nobody wanted to take a seaplane when they had day liberty but that concern died out shortly.

A few weeks later, El Caribe used its insurance money to buy a new aircraft and they were back in business. By then the accident had been nearly forgotten. The airline had no trouble selling tickets. There was always a demand to go island hopping in the Caribbean. One accident was no reason to change that. No reason at all.

Xochicalco

Wind, dry and hot, coursing over
ruins, brown grass rustling,
miniature dust storms spinning.
Beyond, closer, an oval, light blue lake and
further, dry looking mountains, gray and
distant, smoke plumes rising from unknown fires.
Below, the usual ball field, reminder of
ancient ritual, heart sacrifice, knife-wielding priests.
Beside, around, gray-stoned temples, reconstructed,
to feathered serpent god, and about
broken walls of homes, empty now
a millennium and half again.
Nearby, past squat pyramid and
erect, unfathomable stele,
an entrance, a cave, dark and uninviting,
vague light centered, awaiting solar equinox and
brilliant yellow shining beam.
Xochicalco, on leveled hilltop,
life long extinguished, yet remembered,
among the heat and wind of summer,
one hundred fifty decades on.

The Villa at Gaspra

The bright sun glistened bluish-green
on the sea beyond the Villa at Gaspra,
where old Lev had come to recuperate
from another bout with malaria.

Shy, consumptive Anton,
handsome and immaculately dressed,
and dashing, cane-carrying Maxim,
burning with revolutionary zeal,
visited, paid homage to the great master.

Tolstoi, saintly, frail, mutton-chopped and slightly mad
held court on God, Jesus, love and literature.
No more plays, he advised Chekhov,
Shakespeare was bad enough
without you throwing in more.
For Gorki, he challenged: "I'm more a peasant than you,"
then shocked the younger man with
scatological boasts of superior sexual manhood.

After patiently listening to the old man's
explication of the Sermon on the Mount,
the young writers took their respectful leave.

Gorki would have his revolution and survive it, too,
until even fame and reputation could not save him
from the ferocity of the Great Purges.

Chekhov returned to the stage,
despite Tolstoi's admonition,
to his many actresses and to his death,
waiting three years on.

Tolstoi, himself, aged and exhausted,lived beyond Anton,
until slipping into the physical and emotional decline
that ended for him at the station master's home
in distant, nearly forgotten Astapovo.

Through the Pass

From a quarter mile up the side of the volcano,
covered with slippery fine black gravel,
a look back across the land to Ixtaccihuatl,
Popocatepetl's twin, and the pass between.

Through the pass they had come
long centuries before,
Hernan Cortés and his conquistadors,
strange, armor-covered beings,
quickly converting native peoples,
through gift or force,
crossing the country toward Tenochtitlan.

Tenochtitlan, shining Aztec capitol,
land of wealth, culture, religion,
hearts sacrificially torn from chests
to ensure the coming of the next sun.

Yet cowering Tenochtitlan, too,
demi-god Moctezuma
fearful of the return of the white god
Quetzalcoatl, the feathered serpent.

Three hundred metal-plated aliens
out to conquer a mighty nation state
two hundred thousand strong.

The ferocity, the sound of the
conquering destroying army
echoing through time in the distant pass
seen from a quarter mile up Popocatepetl
looking back at the verdant land below
towering, silent Ixtaccihuatl.

Isiolo

Beyond dark, towering Mount Kenya,
past green coffee fields and
busy little villages:
smiling, waving children,
a land grayish brown.

Off the two-lane blacktop road,
dusty ground slaked, cracked,
dry air from seven years drought.

Rattling, banging, flatbed trucks
rumble into Isiolo, on the edge
of the Northern Territory, in the land of
Mau-Mau, Jomo Kenyatta in exile.

Isiolo, dusty, dirty, loud and
overflowing—with cargo lorries,
vendors, camels, and
a strange feeling of uncertainty:
no one in authority,
no rules to obey.

As much Arabia as Africa,
criminal as lawful,
its pulsing heart beating viscerally,
in street, alley and marketplace,
gateway to Samburu,
dirt roads to distant north.

Refilled, the flatbeds roll on,
on into the afternoon, brown clouds rising behind,
away from Isiolo, away from trinket sellers,
boys hawking long, sharp knives,
away—into the fading light of day,
into the uncertainty of coming night.

Hotel Papagayo—Cuernavaca, Mexico

The big neon parrot above
the entrance to the Hotel Papagayo
shone down in muted reds and blues.

Supper a cold cheese sandwich and Corona
at an outdoor table with the
parrot standing colorful guard.

It was Mexico, Day One:
early airport taxi ride; *segundo clase* bus
to Cuernavaca, *la ciudad de la primavera eternal,*
beneath Greene's volcano;
a few blocks walk to hotel.

In bed, later, parrot light
shining across small room in the
warm, liquid night air—doubts,
Doubts, concerns.
Mexico? Why?

Sleep slow arriving, first night far away,
far from familiar, far from home,
yet near another, a new one;
waiting to begin in the bright light
of a new, expectant morn,
outside the watchful eyes of the
Papagayo's parrot, fully subdued,
bland now under the powerful
Cuernavacan sun.

New Year's Eve—Mazatlan

From the second floor patio outside
his room at the Mar del Pacifico,
he heard the sound of the unseen ocean
lapping against old Mazatlan's
crumbling concrete sea wall.

It was New Year's Eve, and
to the north, twenty minutes by city bus,
were new hotels, new bars,
catering to new tourist needs and
college kids down for the holidays.

Life in the old town was slower, quieter—
a good place to wait for a long-expected call.

Downstairs, at the check-in desk, checking again.

"No, *señor*," for the fourth time, nada, nothing yet.
"No problem," he said, "thanks anyway."

Upstairs, New Year's arriving,
an opened bottle of red wine
meant to be shared,
a full glass poured, drained,
another poured.

He went back out onto the patio,
listened to the sea, the softly lapping sea,
its rhythms gentle, monotonous, constant.

Somewhere down the beach to the right
the sound of revelers, the explosion of fireworks.
There was no mistaking this change from old to new,
a *fait accompli.*

Back in the room then, the silent, empty room,
there was no stopping time,
it went on with you or without you,
carried you along—no options,
no going back, only forward,
nothing else could be done.

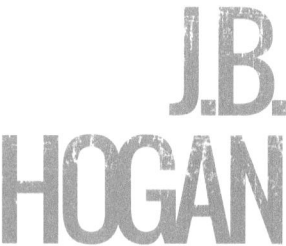

Just His Luck

When I met Ben Vogel he was a year older than me because he repeated the fourth grade.

"Why did you have to do that?" I asked.

"Because they're out to get me."

"Who are they?" I wondered who had it in for nine- and ten-year olds.

"People. Things. Mom says life is out to get me."

"What are you talking about? We're only nine."

"Ten," Ben corrected me.

"How come you had to do fourth grade again?"

"Paper cut."

"A paper cut?"

"Yep."

"Come on. You're making that up."

"Nope. I grabbed a piece of paper and it cut me under my fingernail. Got infected. Almost lost my finger and hand. The doctor cut it to fix it. See?"

I looked at the scar on his left index finger. It was thin, but long.

"Wow." I hadn't ever heard of an infection from a paper cut before.

"There was a red line running all the way down my arm. The doctor said if he hadn't cut it, I could'a died."

"Wow."

"Could'a died," Ben repeated proudly.

I wasn't sure almost dying was something to be all that proud of, but Ben seemed to think so. He saw it, he told me later, as a battle of wills. His against the world, fate—whatever was trying to take him out.

When he was a baby, he had the whooping cough —a disease that had practically disappeared from the developed world—and it nearly killed him. He had been hit by a car on his bicycle, fallen out of a tree on his head and knocked silly, and pulled from a swimming pool just as he was going under for the third time.

In high school and college he had car wrecks and a couple of strange illnesses. And there was also a near fatal accident when a local politician, doing his best impression of a well-known vice-president, discharged a shotgun in Ben's direction.

Finally, Ben adopted a proactive approach. Beat fate to the draw, so to speak. He would become an artist. Draw the scenes of his near-death encounters. Make them realistic and scary, not just for his own good, but also for the edification of an assumed, sympathetic audience. He switched his college major to Art and set about creating artistic representations of how the hostile world was out to get him.

At first, naturally, he failed miserably. His work was viewed as juvenile, petty, perverse, darkly pessimistic. He barely got the grades to graduate, but the artwork seemed to hold off the seemingly inevitable onslaught of bad physical luck. Then one day, a very strange thing happened.

A man in a dark suit came by Ben's studio and purchased one of his paintings. The man had an art gallery, he said. Wanted to sponsor a show of Ben's works, he said. Get his name out, get him some major money.

I went to Ben's opening night at the Touch of Destiny art gallery. He had drawn the paper cut episode on canvas, highlighting, naturally, the long white scar on his finger. There was a stark, black and white pencil sketch of him breaking his knee in a fall and a colorful painting of him hanging in the air like some floating, suffering Jesus *a la* Salvador Dali. Ben sold a lot of paintings. Hooked up with a girl who looked like a supermodel.

"I beat it," he told me, as he left the gallery to find a special bottle of Dom Perignon for the supermodel lookalike. "I'm the master of my fate; I control my own destiny."

"Great," I told him, thinking he shouldn't push his luck too far. "Congratulations."

I went outside to watch him zoom off on a fancy little scooter he just bought. He barely made it around the corner when I heard the crash. Sure enough, not a block away, Ben got hit head on by a bread truck.

I raced to his side and knelt down. I could tell he was done for. I leaned down to hear his final words.

"It's over," he whispered, "they can't do anymore to me now. I won."

"Sure you did, buddy," I closed his eyelids.

The police arrived quickly, took charge of the scene. I gave them a statement and, sighing deeply, looked around. There was a liquor store across the street. They probably had Dom Perignon—and the supermodel would definitely need consoling back at the gallery.

"What the hell," I said, "just his luck, ain't it?"

Sandinista Homes

During the day there were Spanish classes,
in the afternoon political talks.
Afterwards, in the *barrio*, pick up baseball games
played on a rocky, overgrown field.

Early evening would bring a lecture
on local history, neighborhood duties,
heroes of the revolution and maybe
a long walk to what passed for a bar,
with no pitchers and no glasses and
only the national beer.

In the dark of night,
the walk back to Sandinista homes:
little homes in little houses with dirt floors and
huge water bugs but not so much food or water,
yet always just enough electricity
to play the radio and hear,
even from a small cot in a dark
blanket-partitioned room in back,
the sound of popular songs from the north:
songs soft, incongruous, and unexpectedly melancholy.

Dickens in America

1842

Nineteen days on the packet *Brittania* from Liverpool,
nineteen days of the churning, rolling North Atlantic,
making Boston harbor at last, a British re-invasion.

Mr. Dickens, wife and maid, feted, cheered,
celebrated in New York, Philadelphia, Cincinnati, the wild
prairie of distant Illinois.
Traveling on corduroy roads, steamships,
by longed for train.
George Putnam recording all—
both strange and wonderful,
and in Washington, an amiable visit with John Tyler.

But asylums, too, prisons, and Richmond in the south,
abhorrent slavery—the "domestic situation,"
stumping for international protection, copyright laws
protecting all authors, their right to earn.

Suddenly a quick diminishing of welcome,
trip going sour, notes to be developed,
American critique to come.
Last salvo hurled: not the republic
he had come to see, not the one of his imagination.

Retracing the North Atlantic, back home
at last, America safely in the distance
even more fame to come.

1867-1868
Civil war settled, past differences assuaged,
American beckon proffered, the lord of writ returned.
Once more in Boston, the eastern tour repeated,
twenty-five years on,
the western urge restrained.

Full houses everywhere, packed and cheering loud,
five successful months in country,
seventy-six extraordinary performances,
a staggering triumph,
some £20,000 taken in.
Joyous time unparalleled, but
underneath: a crushing truth.
Age coming swiftly, its ails and troubles growing,
the end not far from sight.

One last reading to thunderous applause,
Final reconciliation with the colonies,
home awaiting the ultimate curtain call.

He and America, he told those reporting,
were changed forever more,
slavery gone and author rights improving,
a better place for all.

Both had grown apace, together and afar,
one left to press on into an uncertain future,
the other to the certainty of immortal death.

Storm Over North Africa

Deep into night, most passengers asleep,
through a small, right-side window
of the silent plane, far in the distance
suddenly a light, illuminating the black sky,
giving brief shape to massive thunderhead.

Storm over North Africa,
unimaginable display of power,
backlighting here, then there,
perhaps Tunisia, Libya, Egypt,
very far away, safely away,
a pleasant, comfortable sight.

Like a silent electric movie,
huge flashes behind towering cumulus clouds,
majestic, of no real concern,
only aesthetically pleasing outside
the window of the quiet plane
slicing its way securely through
the dark night.

On the Golf Course

From his seat by the door, R.D. Cross used the bickering of the Sons of Africa defense committee to slip out of the building unnoticed. He headed for the bright lights of downtown. The annoying memory of the hot, smelly committee room occupied his consciousness all the way.

The same old useless plans, he told himself, as he walked along the narrow streets of St. Edward, so ineffectual. They talk a fair match, but nothing happens. Nothing changes. We're a farce. The Sons of Africa. No more than fools.

R.D. passed through a very poor section of town, a small tropical ghetto, its houses of scrap wood and tin, its streets overflowing with refuse and people. Just beyond were several blocks of dingy bars and seedy hotels. R.D. passed the bar hawkers, the pimps, and the working girls without looking up.

He was at home on these streets but they still disgusted him. Ignoring the propositions as he walked along, R.D. felt the anger rising in his blood, the nerves tingling on his back, the feverishness in his head. He hurried along.

As he came near the outer edge of the bar and hotel row, close to his own neighborhood, he paused in front of a flashing, colorful neon sign. In bright reds and greens, the sign advertised:

JACOB'S PAWN SHOP
*SILVER * GUNS * COINS*
TOP DOLLAR

R.D. watched the colors flash off and on for several minutes. They were pleasant to look at but fuzzily distorted. After a few indecisive moments, he pushed open the door and went inside.

—

By nine forty-five the foursome reached the thirteenth tee on the back nine of St. Edward's Oceana Country Club golf course. They were all North Americans. Ted Gianni, fat, balding, overpriced periodontist, Ralph Corzine, stocky, gray-haired banker, Dave Carson, tall, athletic-looking marketing executive, and Tommy Martin, handsome, lean club pro. Each man had a black caddie, local bright-eyed youths, ambitious, hoping to get a good tip.

"What do you say," Ralph boomed from the tee, "a two or a three wood."

"Use the driver, Ralph," Tommy said, "you don't want to play it too short."

Ralph laughed loudly. His shot, a fair hit, traveled about 130 yards and came to rest in good position on the left side of the fairway.

"Good one," Tommy said.

"Way to go, buddy," Ted slapped Ralph's outstretched hand, "good shot."

"Hey, hey," Ralph said. "Last up. Best hit."

"Right," Tommy said.

The group moved down the course towards Ralph's lie. The caddies followed behind.

"They sure keep everything nice here, Tom," Dave waved in the direction of several blue-uniformed young black men tending the course.

"Yes," Tommy said. He noticed one of the workers oddly starting to cross the fairway towards them. "We pride ourselves on that. We feel that when people come down here to play golf, the course should be at least as good as what they left at home, if not better."

"Well, you've done a fine job," Dave commented. "It's great down here."

"It sure is," Ralph added as the club worker continued to approach them.

Dave looked up just as the young man came up next to the group and stopped. He glowered at the golfers.

"Yes?" Tommy asked him. "What is it?"

The youth stepped forward, his right hand in the pocket of his overall uniform.

"I'm R.D. Cross of the Sons of Africa," he said.

The golfers looked at him without understanding.

R.D. pulled his right hand out of his pocket. The caddies dropped their bags and ran. Tommy dove and rolled on the grass. Dave hesitantly moved to his right. Ted and Ralph froze.

"And," R.D. went on quickly, wielding a long barrel .38, "I execute you in the name of the black peoples of St. Edward."

R.D. fired once, striking Dave squarely in the chest. The bullet hit with a thud and blood spurted out of the entry wound. Dave fell straight back, making a low gurgling sound. R.D. fired four more shots with remarkable, deadly accuracy. Ted fell with a hole in his temple, Ralph, a small red spot appearing in the middle of his forehead. The other two shots dropped Tommy and one of the fleeing caddies, but they were not fatal wounds. The remaining caddies, zig zagging across the course, escaped.

The entire episode lasted less than a minute and was strangely, almost preternaturally quiet outside the range of the shooting. To anyone more than a few feet from the scene, the only sound they would have heard was the sharp report of R.D.'s .38. The men died with so little fuss.

R.D. emptied his last round into one of the golf bags that lay, clubs askew, near the dead and wounded men. He was done. He pocketed the weapon and calmly walked away.

As he made his way through the streets adjacent to the club, he heard the wail of sirens but paid them no mind. He walked on quietly. He felt a great weight had been lifted from his body. He thought of the defense committee and smiled to think how they would have to deal with the police and the papers. He pictured them scrambling to deny him, to deny he was a member of the inner circle of the Sons of Africa. He laughed out loud.

His path led away from downtown, toward the ocean. As he went, R.D. thought about the shooting, how strange it was, how easy, how the men died so quietly—with hardly a struggle. He thought of his family and how he had freed them. He felt very good and proud of himself.

He thought of the Sons of Africa again, how he did the work they would not. He told himself that when action was required he had taken it. He had not merely stood by and let things happen anymore. He had intervened. He had acted. He had solved.

Yet, as he reached the soft, sandy shore and heard the small waves breaking lightly, something still nagged at him. Some doubt about something gnawed at the back of his consciousness. Looking down, he saw the remains of a small bird, its body speckled lightly with blood and partly split and torn. But not eaten. And then he thought once more of the men on the golf course. He saw their blood spilled on the finely manicured grass. He saw them sprawled awkwardly on the ground. Dead and dying.

A strange sound started in R.D.'s throat then, involuntarily at first. He felt it push its way up from inside himself, stronger than his will to suppress it. He realized he had begun to laugh. It was hardly different than crying. He tried to stop but couldn't. It made him feel out of control, as if he were a third party to his own life. As if the laughter came from somewhere else, from someone else.

He struggled harder to stop the sound, but it would not stop. He felt it spread over and through his body, removing his cares, freeing him. He walked forward, and finally, at the last, felt himself cleansed, purified, washed deep inside. He walked forward, further and further, until he floated free, numb to the past and the future, submerged in the final now. Free at the very end. At last.

Feeling Gray

I'm seeing gray, feeling gray,
      thinking
      touching
      smelling
      hearing
      relating
to gray.

And I'm about to lose it,
six-thirty is too damned early
to be
in this lousy bus place.

The obscurity is making
me ill;
all those faces with no names,
names with no faces,
going to places I
never want to be.

Good Friday—León, Nicaragua

Torn, peeling signs still posted everywhere,
Some two years after the papal visit;
religious fervor permeates the streets of León
in delayed echo of El Papa's pastoral trip.
Thousands throng avenue and alley,
marching to a mock Golgotha, a faux Jesus,
replete with cringing duo of thieves,
driven through town by rope-whipping Romans,
booed incessantly by the following crowd,
wailing, moaning re-enactors in their midst
Christ pushed and shoved along to Calvary field
beside the road filled with gawkers and true believers,
Jesus and the thieves, crying out for mercy,
standing on wooden blocks,
nailed to the bottom of wooden crosses,
the Lord—always in character—extending his arms:
"Oh, Señor, por qué me has abandonado?"
Savior dead at last, ceremony done,
a slowly dispersing crowd

back to home, restaurant, tourist bus—
back to Managua, where
religion is officially frowned upon
by the Sandinista government,
and perhaps by others wishing
there was something else to do on
Good Friday in León, Nicaragua.

Red Brick House

She was nearly as old
as the red brick house
where she lived and
she was a proper, old-fashioned lady,
a widow with a son and
daughter-in-law who dutifully, reluctantly,
checked on her once a week,
but it was her grandson Kevin,
she cared about.

He visited her almost every day and
she made him little finger sandwiches and
chocolate milk with real cocoa and
when his pals visited she treated them like
they actually belonged in her house
instead of being mostly poor boys
from the wrong side of town.

Many years later the
red brick house was still there
where the little grandmother
and her grandson had been—
both gone many years now—
all that seemed left was the
emptiness of life, vanity of hope,
loss of youthful days, the long past hard to hold onto,
fading further each day into the
depths of diminishing, unremembered memory.

Orphan

Cold mist drifting down
floating onto gravestones,
coating them with a silvery sheen.
In back, beyond the last graves, a
huge oak tree, leafless,
limbs gnarled, bark as gray as the
dull sky above.

Nearer, graves of great-aunts and uncles,
nearly-forgotten faces vaguely recalled, and
closer still the closer ones—grandparents,
sisters and brothers of mothers and fathers,
all gone now, lives echoing only in memory,
joy, pain, all struggles over now.

And closest yet, mother, father,
empty places in heart and mind,
gone now, nor flesh nor touch
never felt again,
the empty, unfilled places,

not to be filled, ever,
solo then, without parent,
alone for the rest of time,
time's child, time's orphan.

To Stop a Cockfight

They went down to Cuba by themselves,
avoiding the usual emotional hangers-on,
to soak up the ambience maybe
or to dry him out or soak up more
alcohol or self-pity or whatever it was
they liked to soak in—
he for his writing, she for her art.

She was still recovering
from yet another nervous collapse
that his drinking, philandering, and more drinking
did little to stave off.

They went to the Floridita and drank where
they and Papa used to drink and stayed in a fine hotel
and got themselves a driver who knew where
all the good stuff was hidden in those hot
sultry Havana nights and he told the driver
to take them where the action was.

The driver pulled up to a Gallera,
opened the doors for them.
The experience they sought lay within
the driver insisted, beyond that green door
over there.

Inside it was a madhouse.
Perfect for her. It made her feel normal.
The bettors were yelling, their birds squawking,
Chicken blood flying.

They were in trouble right away.
She flirted ostentatiously with the men,
he laughed and leered suggestively.

When the first cock was cut,
when its back legs were sliced and
dangling uselessly, she cried,
screamed at him to stop the fight.

Gallantly, he strode toward the ring
demanded an end to the slaughter,
argued with the gamblers, the officials,
threw a bottle at the cocks.

In a heartbeat, the gamblers were on him
kicking, hitting, beating him nearly senseless.

She cried at the violence, tried to rescue him,
was pushed aside roughly.

Luckily the driver intervened,
drug them out of the place, apologized,
dropped them at a hospital.

Inside, she worried his battered, once handsome face,
begged help for him, got him a room.

After, she went back stateside without him,
resumed her treatment.
He was flown home to a hospital,
to dry out and recover.

For the next eighteen months they exchanged letters
but they never saw each other again.
Then one day his overtaxed heart simply gave up.
She may or may not have cried, no one could tell,
she completed her treatment, made a new life for herself,
never once looked back.

Down from the Country Club

"Don't you have any hamburgers?" the woman demanded in English.

"*Señora?*" the vendor stared at the woman's extravagant wedding ring and then at the sun tan oil glistening on her soft, white belly.

She was staying at El Caribe where all the wealthy Americans stayed. The vendor had seen her sunbathing just outside the Caribe's chain link fence.

"Hamburgers, hamburgers. Don't you understand English?"

"*Oh, sí,*" the vendor pulled a couple of tinfoil-wrapped hot dogs out of his cart and held them up. Hot dogs, hamburgers, it was all the gringos ate. The old man figured they were pretty much the same.

"For God's sake," the woman snapped, "those are hot dogs, not hamburgers. Why don't you people bother to learn a little English?"

"*No es okay?*"

"Why me?" the woman dug in her change purse, "of all the vendors."

A local boy in his late teens came up to the cart and stood beside the woman. She looked at him and frowned.

"Dame dos coca," he said to the vendor.

"I was here first," the woman extracted some bills from her purse. The boy leaned back, surprised.

"Oy," he laughed. The vendor gave him a stern look.

"Give me the hot dogs," the woman held up two fingers. "Two. *Dos.*" The boy winked at the vendor.

"Sí, señora," the vendor said. *"Dos."*

He handed the hot dogs to her. She pushed the money at him. He counted it and tried to give her one bill back.

"Demasiado," he said, then in broken English, "too much *señora*. You pay too much. *Uno."* The boy giggled.

"No," the woman barked, as much to the boy as to the vendor. "Keep it. It's yours. Yours."

"Gracia, señora," the vendor said politely, *"mucha gracia."*

"Dos coca," the boy stepped up close to the woman.

"Well . . . ." she huffed, moved away. The boy laughed. The vendor handed him his drinks.

"No la moleste," the older man said sharply, "don't bother her."

"Calma, viejo," the boy said, "relax."

The woman stalked away, back across the beach towards El Caribe. The boy paid for the sodas.

"Bruja," he said in the direction of the woman, *"bruja gorda.* Fat witch."

The vendor closed the cart lid and ran a grizzled hand through his gray, receding hair. He watched the white *gringa* lady walk back to El Caribe, back behind its chain link fence. He scratched the stubbly growth on his chin and squinted into the sun. His face betrayed no reaction. He might as well have been wearing a mask.

Nairobi

Within marketplace—
showy trinkets, tourist cups and spoons,
without—raw, plucked chickens for sale,
chunks of fly-covered red meat heating in the
buzzing, humid-hot air.

At the edges, hawkers and hustlers roam,
and the lame, the ill,
cripples wheeling past on medieval carts.

Loud, bustling streets beyond
filled with walkers,
everyone walking,
men holding hands Kenyan style.

Circling traffic roundabouts,
indecipherable lights on corners,
past a sandy, weedy golf course,
up a hill past luxuriant hotels,
an odd pervasive smell,
odor of burning refuse,
ubiquitous, unpleasantly sweet.

On the road out of town,
Impalas play along the highway
like stray dogs wandering
beside ineffectual fences surrounding
international factories and plants.

Two-lane blacktop highway to the south
cutting through the desert-like land,
with Arizona feel and look,
running to the great game preserves,
to the sunny playground of the coast,
leaving Nairobi, loud and overflowing,
in the silent distance behind.

It's Hard to Imagine You as a Woman

It's hard to imagine you as a woman
your sword is so sharp
your armor so hard.

And the way you walk and talk.

Like a banty rooster servicing a hen
like a general commanding his troops from a jeep
like a Baptist preacher railing at his flock.

How could such a magnificent lady,
face shining with good will,
breasts swollen with pride,
hips supporting the weight of the future,
turn out this way?

Now, these many years later
it's still hard to imagine you a woman
hips spread too close to the ground,
breasts sagging to the waist,
and the face—such a face.

Who could recognize in the gray, drooping flesh
  the dull, unfocused eyes
the gem you once were?

The gem I longed to possess
the gem I longed to hold—and touch
the gem whose transparent beauty brooked
no false descriptions,
no hard armor,
and no sharp swords,
masculinely hot and unthinking.

poetry

Reading Don Quixote—
San Miguel de Allende

One-room apartment on Avenida Mesones
at the top of a narrow flight of stairs;
single bed, table and two chairs, small kitchen with
pan for making spaghetti, and in the refrigerator—
half a bottle of red wine, package of Hershey kisses.
Not so far from the tracks where
Cassaday fell, his heart played out,
no one much remembers now.
Across the little pueblo, language schools,
students spilling out to
clubs, bars, art galleries.
Inside, a copy of Don Quixote,
resting all day on the table,
in the quiet, away from the noise, the
bustle of life on old cobblestone streets,
wine and chocolate waiting, the presence of
Cervantes, cool, modern Cervantes,
"What giants?" incredulous Sancho cries.

Smooth Cervantes, comic, good-hearted,
Book II a response to critics, doubters,
literary pleasure near non-pareil,
all casually perused and enjoyed
above the busy cobblestone streets
of rare, distant San Miguel de Allende.

Locked Turnstile and Barbed Wire

Six-fifteen a. m. pitch dark,
empty parking lot save
three cars and one,
frosty breath and pricks of
cold on ears.
Orion lowering in the distant sky,
tall turnstile in front,
no others near, no sound,
lonely in the cold, anticipating
warmth inside, light, heat,
work station at the ready,
cafeteria stroll for
juice and bagel past
occasional office lit, early bird working;
but first the badge reader—
click in, push through turnstile
past the fence lined with barbed wire,
to keep someone out, in?
Up stairs to double doors,
pause between inside, out;

turn, resigned, let doors shut,
slam behind, move forward,
solitary steps echoing
in the empty hallway.

Ice Storm

Liquid silver sheet falling,
falling day and night, gray and black,
limbs draped in crystalline ice.

Hour by hour, weight increasing,
creaking arms spread, lowered, dropped.

Loud snaps follow,
thunderous breaks, brilliant sheen
over all—ground, shrub, tree.

Unrelenting, falling still,
trees uprooted, roofs battered,
all movement stopped.

Dark then, bitter cold,
no sound save popping, cracking,
heavy wet logs thudding on rigid earth.

No venturing out, nothing to do,
fearsome beauty to be admired,
awesome power beheld.

Bright shining return at last,
hoar-coat lessening, yet still
explosive, crashing, world slowly,
carefully re-emerging,
peering about amid low whistles,
mumbled, stuttered curses.

Images all left at end
of devastation keen,
beyond recent memory,
like a war lost or misremembered,
one without enemy or purpose,
its only casualties security, comfort,
an easy peace of mind.

Hurricane

Sometime before dawn, the first rain came. In steady, driving torrents it hammered on roofs, filled drainpipes, overtaxed gutters. It came in wind-whipped, jalousy-rattling sheets battering the walls and windows of the apartment Dan McGuire shared with his Boca Tierran girlfriend Gabriela "Gabi" Solis.

While Gabi confirmed that they had several days of canned groceries stored up, Dan fiddled with an old radio, trying to find a weather report.

"Have you heard anything yet?" Gabi asked.

"No. I can't seem to find a good station. I want to know if this thing is going to get really bad."

He adjusted the dial again. Finally, he found a stronger signal. The announcer gave the weather.

"Hot damn. Got it."

"What's he saying?"

"Listen," Dan said, "maybe you can catch it."

They concentrated until the announcer moved on to another topic.

"He said big waves and a lot of rain," Gabi said.

"Yeah. I thought he said something about seventy-five to a hundred miles from somewhere. I didn't get the rest."

"Maybe that's how close it is to us now."

"Hmm, could be. If that's it, we may still be in for it."

"May be."

"Well, it's not here yet," Dan said, "what do you say we eat something."

"Like what?"

"Oh, I don't know. How about cheese sandwiches and Cokes."

"Yech."

"Well, I don't know then. What do you want?"

"I don't know," Gabi said. "How about chicken from the Pio-Pio?"

"Pio-Pio. I'm not going out for chicken."

"Okay, I'll make something here."

While Gabi began preparing the food in the apartment's little kitchen, Dan stood at the back door and watched the rain falling in the back yard. He felt the cool air and the mist from the rain as it came through the louvres on the door and was scattered, minutely, into the air. He liked watching and feeling the rain and he stood at the door for several minutes. Finally, he turned away and went to the kitchen to help Gabi.

—

The winds and rain lasted for three days but the hurricane never came. It went north of Boca Tierra missing the island by many miles. For Dan and Gabi the battered plants and inundated back yards and muddy running gutters in the neighborhood were the only tangible evidence of the storm.

"Wasn't much of a hurricane, was it?" Dan tossed a three-pack of flan into the grocery cart at the Isla Grande supermarket.

"I guess not," Gabi agreed, eyeing the very rich flan sideways, "but we were probably really lucky."

"I suppose." But it sure wimped out after all the buildup. All it did was make everything really wet. Big deal."

In the checkout line a few minutes later, Gabi thumbed through a copy of the daily San Sebastian Star, the island's only English language newspaper.

"Dan," she said, "look at this. It says there was a bunch of people killed in the storm."

"Killed? Killed? How?"

"In the storm. Look."

Dan took the paper and scanned the front page. Twelve persons had drowned in flooding caused by the huge storm system that passed by Boca Tierra.

The dead were all farm people. *Campesinos* whose houses of cheap wood and scrap tin—built squatter style into the side of jungle hollows—were swept away by flash floods rushing off jungle hills in the interior.

Centered on page one was a graphic photograph of

local authorities pulling the bloated body of a woman from a muddy, swollen stream. Dan handed the paper back to Gabi.

"You want to get it?" she asked.

"I don't know."

"I'll put it back."

"No, don't. I hadn't thought about anything like this, that's all. It never occurred to me."

"No," Gabi said. The checker totaled their bill.

"I never thought about something like this," Dan repeated.

"You haven't lived here very long, baby," Gabi gently reminded him. "How would you know?"

"Whew." Dan shook his head. "There's a lot of stuff I don't know."

"*Seis, ochenta y siete,*" the checker said. "Six dollars and eighty-seven cents."

Gabi handed him the money. He rang up the sale.

Baboon Cliffs

From Baboon Cliffs, Lake Nakuru
floated in the distance, elliptical,
steel gray, pink-circled with Flamingos
motionless at first, then suddenly
alive on the edges and
in the air above becoming
pink, too, but silent from afar.
Down below, under the
cliffs—baboons, gray-brown,
quick-moving, sure-footed, silent,
and fat hyrax, rodent-like
light gray, skittering here,
there, chunky little herbivores.
Out on the plains, calm waterbuck,
giraffe, hippo and beyond,
at the hazy horizon, low white
clouds float by bathing the
land in cool, rolling shadow.

Open Casket

The coffin was open but
I tried not to look.
I'd seen him out of the corner
of my eye when I walked into
the little church where they
were having his funeral.

I don't know if he'd ever been
in a church before.
I only went into them when
there was a funeral,
why would I?

His middle son gave the sermon
and a good one,
especially considering who
the old man was, had been.

He was drunken, railroad
Irish and a hard, tough man,
who his oldest son still loved and
maybe his one daughter, too.

Outside in the little cemetery
they buried him in the cold and wind
but that didn't make my eyes tear up
because I had never really known him,
you see, my whole life had been with
my mother and he always knew I
was my mother's son, and that
I was never really his.

Time Became an Arrow

Along roadway power lines
memories echo still,
memories old but not forgotten,
resonating in the chill air.

Memories once alive, vibrant,
expectant of expected dreams;
casual dreams desired,
deferred until tomorrow in the
pleasure of today.

On time's cusp then,
no thought of future,
not counting yesterdays.

But time became an arrow,
shot hard and fast and true,
shaft piercing promises—
point slicing plans and dreams.

New choices then required, unwanted,
new accommodations, new work.
Resisting failure and unstoppable time,
death of hope and ideal.

Absorbing past into present,
tomorrow beckons, needing
strength and clarity,
firm vision, unwavering hand.

Past not forgotten, today lived in full,
facing future calmly, its promise
never surrendered, its possibility
never denied.

Semenovski Square

Was a blanket of snow,
the frozen air filled with icy breath
of horse and soldier—and the condemned.

On the scaffolding, Feodor stood,
all Saint Petersburg before him,
white, cold, distant.

Below, tied to wooden stakes,
unrepentant, unhooded Petrashevski,
poor Mombelli, fragile Grigoriev,
waited, waited, rifles aimed at their heads.

Above, Feodor, next in line, sought peace
from agitation, the certainty of impending death,
in reconciliation, accommodation,
saw sunlight flash on church steeple beyond,
flashing light of uncertainty, of terrible truth,
of final, unknowable mystery.

But then, the roll of drums,
 the prayer of prayers answered,
the reprieve, the benevolence of kind Nicholas,
the prisoners unbound, the true sentence read.

Grigoriev hence mad, Petrashevski defiant still,
Feodor in transports of relief, the years of exile to come
a prickly balm for his epileptic soul,
a seething fire for his raging ambition,
the incandescent spark for his explosive genius.

Southern Hospitality

"Gimme a hamburger, fries and a Coke," Baker told the teenager behind the counter at Wilbur's Drive-In.

"I'm sorry, sir," the boy squeaked, voice wavering, "we're closed."

Baker wobbled against the counter and leaned over it. The boy backed away, grimacing fearfully. Baker was a big, thick Pennsylvania boy and he was drunk as hell. He could be pretty scary. A couple of young girls and another boy working at the grill and soda fountain several feet behind the counter watched the scene unfold. Another kid was off to the side but neither Baker, nor Owens, who stood behind Baker laughing, noticed what he was doing.

"I guess you didn't hear me, sonny," Baker gestured towards the boy, "I want a burger, fries, and a Coke. So does my buddy here. Now hop to it." The boy didn't move.

"Just cook us some food fast and we'll be out of here before you know it," Owens interjected.

"We can't, sir," the timid boy said to Owens, "we really

are closed, and the boss will get real mad if we stay open longer."

"The hell with your boss," Baker threatened, "get your butt back there and get us some chow, mister. Move it."

The boy backed up another step but still faced Baker and Owens. He was scared, but he wasn't going to get in trouble with the boss. One of the young girls by the grill, a curly-haired blonde came up to the counter.

"Why don't you guys go on back to the base," she said evenly. "We're closed and you're trespassing here." As she spoke, a black and white cruiser pulled into Wilbur's parking lot with its lights off.

"Trespassing," Baker laughed drunkenly, "you hear that Owens. We're trespassing, in a lousy burger joint in Crapland, North Carolina." He guffawed. Owens chuckled, but not too much. The curly-haired blonde girl was very cute.

"All we want's some food here," Owens told the girl, "we're hungry and we want to eat before we go back to the base."

"Please leave," the girl said. "We're not going to reopen and you're trespassing on our property."

"Damn it," Baker banged his hand on the counter, making both the girl and the timid boy jump, "you better..."

"What's the problem here," a deep voice in back of Baker and Owens suddenly boomed.

They turned to see a stocky local cop standing behind them, arms folded across his considerable chest. Wilbur's kids excitedly gathered around the cash register.

"You boys causing a little ruckus, are you?"

Baker grunted. Owens tried to be cool.

"No, sir," he said, the "sir" coming out of his system like a string of bilious phlegm, "we were just trying to get something to eat. We thought they were still open."

"We told them we were closed," the timid boy volunteered.

Baker gave the kid a fierce look over his shoulder. The kid backed up two or three steps.

"That's right," the blonde said, "but they wouldn't leave."

"All right, boys," the cop said, "let's go."

"Go where?" Baker said brusquely. "What'd we do?"

"Officer," Owens said, "it's a mistake. We'll leave. We're just heading back to base."

"Let's go," the cop said.

"What are you talking about?" Baker moved towards the cop. The cop put his hand on his night stick.

"Donny, Donny," Owens intervened, stepping between Baker and the cop, "cool it."

"Let's go," the cop said.

Outside by the police car with the Wilbur's kids watching from inside, the cop cuffed Baker, then Owens. He put them in the back seat. All the way downtown, Baker maintained a running complaint. The cop nearly stopped the car a couple of times.

"What are we?" Baker repeatedly griped in more or less the same words, "Murderers? Killers? All we wanted was some lousy ass food."

"Shut your mouth, boy," the cop told Baker, repeatedly.

"Knock it off, Donny," Owens said each time Baker opened his yap, "shut up."

But Baker kept up his rant, getting even louder when the cop would turn around and threaten to shut him up. After a while, Owens just slumped in the corner, too tired and too drunk himself to keep up with the battle. At the police station, the cop hustled them up to the Desk Sergeant's counter.

"Here you go, Rafe," the cop told the sergeant, "got a couple of heroes here. This big one's a real wise guy, ain't you, boy?"

He pushed Baker against the counter to emphasize his point. Baker mumbled something.

"Speak up," the sergeant said.

When the sergeant talked, Owens realized for the first time what people were talking about when they called somebody a red neck. The corpulent cop's neck was in fact red, the veins sticking out grossly as he talked.

"Well," he said, "what was it? You got a grievance?"

Baker muttered under his breath.

"Empty your pockets," the sergeant said.

The arresting officer and a couple of other cops standing behind Owens and Baker laughed at the proceedings. But when they apparently felt Owens was too slow in responding, they grabbed his front pockets from behind and pulled up hard, the seams on his jeans pinching hard at his groin.

"All right, all right," he said, hurrying to empty his pockets, "I'm doing it. I'm doing it. It ain't easy with these cuffs on."

The cops laughed again. They seemed to think they were very funny.

After they got Owens squared away, the officers pushed Baker down a narrow hall in back. Baker was having none of it and a brief scuffle broke out. Owens moved quickly into the hall to see what was happening but two of the cops grabbed him and slammed him up against the wall.

"Don't move," one of them snarled.

Owens went rigid. Down the corridor, the police subdued Baker and hustled him into the cells in back of the station. The other cops released Owens and shoved him down the hallway. He made a point of not resisting them.

There were only five large cells in the jail, all concrete and bars, completely bare but clean. They were empty except for a couple of guys in one cell and a solitary passed out drunk in the cell where they put Owens and Baker.

Their cell had three metal bunk beds without mattresses, sheets, or pillows. There were no facilities. After he was uncuffed, Owens went to a lower bunk opposite the drunk and sat down. The arresting cop hadn't uncuffed Baker yet. The other cops went back up front.

"Gimme your hands, boy," the cop told Baker. "Move it."

"Go to hell," Baker said.

"Shut up, Donny," Owens stood up.

"Sit down," the cop told him. Owens didn't sit down. "Couple of tough guys, huh?"

"Go to hell," Baker said.

The cop slapped him open handed, hard. Owens moved forward. The cop pointed at him. Owens stopped.

"Butthole," Baker opened and closed his cuffed hands at his waist. The cop slapped him again, really hard.

"Bastard." He got slapped again and again.

"Donny," Owens said, "shut the hell up."

"Motherfucker," Baker said.

The cop slapped him three times, very hard. Baker's face was bright red all over. His eyes watered involuntarily and blazed with anger. He looked like a madman ready to kill. But he didn't say anything else. The cop laughed. Owens sat down on a metal bunk. The cop leered at Baker for a few moments more, then roughly uncuffed him. Baker wobbled backwards.

"Get you some sleep, boys," the cop stepped out of the cell and closed it loudly behind him. "We'll make your call for you. I'm sure your commander will be real glad to send some boys out to pick you up, real glad."

"Jesus Christ, Donny," Owens said after the cop was gone, "you could've got yourself beat half to death."

"Screw 'em,' Baker climbed onto a top bunk, "they can go to hell."

"Lousy beds," Owens complained, "they're like sleeping on an airplane wing."

"Stupid southern rednecks. Some treatment, huh?"

"Southern hospitality," Owens said.

Baker thought that was funny. He laughed until the combination of the night's events—the alcohol, the arrest, being slapped around—caught up to him and his laughter turned into a barking cough that sounded like somebody throwing up.

"Jesus, Baker," Owens said, "settle down, dude."

"Yeah." Baker spluttered.

"I'm goin' to sleep," Owens gingerly laid his head on the hard metal, "if I can."

"Guess we're gonna get it for this one, huh?"

"S'pose so," Owens yawned.

It was after three in the morning when the base police came for Owens and Baker. They weren't particularly hostile and their mild threats about base punishment didn't bother the two young GIs. Baker was now totally docile and sat beside Owens in back of the covered jeep with his eyes closed not saying a word. Owens was surprised at how sober he felt and that Baker's face wasn't all bruised up. He even exchanged a few words with the cops up front.

As they drove through the deserted town, through the black night and chill air, Owens smiled. Maybe for the first time since he'd been in the service, he actually found himself looking forward to getting back on base.

It was indeed a new sensation for him and he almost laughed out loud. One look at the military cops, however, with their fuzz cuts and rigid jaws, and he suppressed that impulse. He knew you didn't press your luck too often with the police, civilian or otherwise. It was a lesson he'd been slow to learn, but he was beginning to get a handle on it. He leaned against the side of the jeep and sighed. Baker looked like he was asleep. The jeep rattled on towards the base.

I Thought I Heard

Emily Dickinson buzz when I died,
but how could I be sure
with all those other voices clamoring,
competing for the last thought?
as anyone i had lived in a pretty how town
with up so floating many bells down alright,
but I was still compelled to rage, rage
against the dying of the light,
even when I stood beyond my good neighbor's fence
with so many miles to go before I slept.
What does it mean, mister, I wondered
when a man crashes out?
Does it mean I was there where Ma could
look at me and see I've made it—top of the world?
Yet I had not gone into the deep two-hearted river
fishing for the depths of my soul
nor plucked Dewey Dell's fecund jewel;
the grave's a fine and private place,
I reasoned, but still I hoped to go out
with a bang and not a whimper.

Oh, death, I said, I see thou sting,
but let me see the sun rise
just one more time.
Yet, I didn't hear a fly buzz
when I died but the hiss
of the fly crashing out in a
glorious final flash of man-made
lightning in the backyard
electronic insect killer.

Anecdote of the Jaw: Wallace Stevens and a Large Puddle of Water

February 1936, long, tall,
over-weight and middle-aging
Wallace Stevens, most excellent insurance company poet,
having exhausted his latest traditional spat
with Mr. Robert Frost, sought out bigger game,
at an upscale Key West soiree.

Drinking too much, as was his wont,
the executive bard trash-mouthed
the great Papa bear in company
of baby sister bear Ursula
and made her cry—all the way home
to big brother.

Confronted on the street by Papa, 36,
the actuarial verse-smith, 56, put dukes up,
swung wildly at the shorter, stocky man.
Papa, in a testosterone fit, wiped up
the wet street with the taller, heavier

word-worker—sending him sprawling
into a puddle of water.
Up came swinging, the big modernist icon,
his fist catching Papa's jaw flush,
and shattering itself, and not the bear's jaw,
in two distinct places.

Down again went Wallace, faster than Max Schmeling,
and again, until he was so beaten, bloody, and battered,
the large bear took pity and stopped.

No reason to tell anybody about this, Mr. Stevens,
the loser, suggested to his literary over-match.
None whatsoever, agreed Papa,
although nice letters to Dos Passos and Mrs. Murphy,
revealed the joy and pride he took in pounding
the daylights out of the sometimes drunkenly obnoxious
past his prime insurance company vice-president poet.

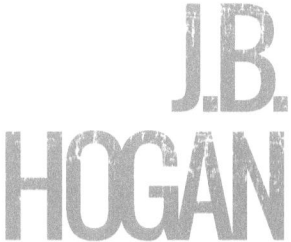

A Small Concussion

The Boy's Club gym was so bright coming in out of the late December night I had to squint to see. And it was so warm inside it made me sleepy. I tagged along behind my brother Dave as we walked along the side of the basketball court. Out in the middle of the court was the boxing ring, set up for tonight's fights. There were foldout chairs on three sides of the ring and there was a good crowd already.

We looked for our brother Jim but it wasn't his fight yet. Jim was a really good boxer. Our sister, Mary, kept a scrap book and pasted all the newspaper clippings about Jim's Boy's Club and Golden Gloves fights in it. The stories liked to mention that Jim would smile at his opponents when they hit him real hard. They said it was like Jim was showing the other guy that whatever he hit Jim with, it didn't hurt.

Dave and I worked our way to some seats about three rows back where we had a good straight on look at the ring. The other fight was in the third and final round and was a pretty good one but we were all excited for it to get over and it to be Jim's turn.

Lately Jim had some trouble because in one fight he took too many punches and had what our doctor said was a small concussion. Before Jim had the small concussion he used to play a game with us after his fights. He would come home hanging his head and looking all sad and then just about the time we would all be saying how that was too bad and he'd do better next time, he'd break out grinning and holler out: "I won." Then the whole family would yell and cheer and jump around and hug him and stuff.

It was a lot of fun, but since the small concussion Jim stopped doing that. Win or lose, his head hurt too much to joke around. Our mother wanted him to stop fighting till he got completely well but Jim wouldn't have none of that. That would have been too sissy he said. So he kept fighting with his head hurt and mom asked me and Dave to go tonight to make sure Jim was okay and come home with him after the fight.

After a few minutes break it was time for Jim's fight. The first round went okay. Jim moved in and out, kept his left jab in the guy's face, bobbed, danced, landed a few good rights. The other guy stayed with him pretty well, even landing a pretty good left hook which brought Jim's famous "you didn't hurt me" smile to his face.

All in all it was a good round with Jim maybe taking it 10-9 if you were judging on the ten-point must system. But in the second all heck broke loose.

They had fought about a minute into the round, when the other guy managed to slip in a hard left jab followed by a really strong left hook. We were expecting Jim to get that smile on his face again and punch his way out of trouble but what happened caught everyone, especially the guy in the ring with Jim, off guard.

The guy's punches must've hurt Jim's head, hurt his concussion. You could see the pain and anger in Jim's eyes and then they glazed over, real scary like, and he went after the guy like a mad animal or something.

Jim threw punches so fast and hard it took your breath away. There was a roar from the crowd and Dave whistled and say something like "man, oh, man."

Jim threw punch after punch: left jabs, uppercuts, and a whistling left hook that dropped the guy. The ref had to push Jim away to do the count. The other boy got up at eight, let the ref wipe off his gloves and then it started again.

Jim flew at him and knocked his mouthpiece out. The boy slumped over but Jim held him up and kept punching until the ref got between them. Jim lunged forward anyway and knocked the guy down. The guy barely beat the ten-count and the ref had to push Jim away again to keep him from hitting the boy when he was down.

Jim's very first punch after the count rocked the guy again and he feebly tried to cover up. Jim cut loose with everything he had. Lefts, rights, uppercuts, jabs, hooks. Finally the other guy stumbled, fell backwards and for just a second one of his knees grazed the canvas.

In his mad way Jim slugged the boy so hard he drove him right through the ropes and out of the ring onto the first row of spectators. The place went wild. Dave yelled and yelled. I may have been the only one quiet in the whole club. I was so scared I just shut up completely. The crowd roared.

At first the ref held up Jim's hand, ruling it a TKO. Jim's seconds rushed into the ring and led him back to his corner. The other guy's people helped him back into the ring. He had no idea where he was. Then something started happening. The ref was talking to the judges. You couldn't hear them but you knew something was up and that it probably wouldn't be good.

The ref hollered something over to Jim's corner that really got his seconds stirred up. Then the ref went over to the other boy's corner and held up his hand in victory. The crowd booed. The other boy was still out of it but Jim, even in his blinding pain, understood he'd been disqualified for hitting the guy when he was down.

As the crowd got quieter, we could hear Jim yelling at the ref. He was cursing. Now I had heard Jim curse before. When I was five, he was punching holes in the lid of a can and put an ice pick through that fleshy web between your thumb and forefinger. I heard plenty of bad words that time you bet, but they were nothing compared to what he put together now.

Swearing at the top of his voice and pointing at the ref and at the beat up guy, Jim was hustled out of the ring by his seconds before he got himself in big trouble. I remember watching them lead Jim away from the ring, away from me and Dave, out across the gym floor.

At the end of the gym closest to us, there was a stairway that led to the locker room. Jim's seconds took him towards the stairs as fast as they could. All the while, Jim kept up his cursing. For a moment, when they got him to the stairway and helped him up to the second floor, you couldn't hear anything. When they reappeared, Jim was still yelling at the ref and he kept it up until they got him into the locker room.

In the excitement, I somehow lost Dave. I remember staring at the closed locker room door up on the second floor and feeling like I was completely alone in the building. I had never seen anything like that – either the fight or what happened after. A couple of minutes later Dave reappeared at my side.

"C'mon," he said, "let's go."

"We're not gonna watch anymore fights?" I asked stupidly, as if I really wanted to.

"No, c'mon."

"We gonna tell mom?"

"Tell her what? Besides, she's at work."

"Oh, yeah."

"You ain't gonna say nothin' about what happened, are you?" Dave asked. I didn't say anything right away. "Well?"

"Heck no," I said. "I won't."

"You better not."

"I said I wouldn't."

"Okay. Let's go home."

"Ain't we gonna wait for Jim?"

"No, he's too mad for that. We better stay out of his way."

"Oh," I said.

Outside it was very dark and the cold wind whipped right through our worn jackets. We hustled away from town and down the big hill that bottomed out three or four blocks from our house. I remember having this empty feeling in me as we walked home. Empty like the hungriest you ever been or empty like maybe a hole was where your heart used to be or something.

I hadn't ever felt that way before and it made me want to walk faster in the chill night air. I was glad Dave was with me and I hung by his side, quiet, hurrying my steps to keep up, not saying anything else, not one word, all the rest of the way home.

Inoperative

Somewhere back there
among the Tel-Stars
and the "Ram-a-Lama-Ding-Dongs,"
god was rendered inoperative.

In the new absence,
reborn heathens grew up and
seized pagan gods, or
just grew old, and
left worshipping to children.

poetry

El Coral

Buses belching black smoke
on the highway out of Managua
overflowing with riders, some on roof,
others dangling from doors
we followed in a newer school bus,
foreigners, turistas, international workers
headed for the countryside, green, fertile, third world
of one-lane roads past farms
and little thrown together homes.

It was on to El Coral
with its Saturday afternoon rodeo and then
a young Sandinista soldier,
AK-47 strapped to his back, there to protect
against the Contra threat,
warnings and counter-warnings plastered on
schools, trees, and an outbuilding
passing for a way station and restaurant—
in back an old-time outhouse guarded
by two massive, snorting pigs.

In the center of the little pueblito a band,
traditional local music,
the men not smiling, a little boy maybe ten years old
playing guitar and singing.

Later, a political argument,
then piling back onto the bus for Managua
ruffled feelings slightly raw,
the vehicle chugging away at last,
back to Managua, dark and quiet at night,
full moon shining down on the silent, apprehensive and
hopefully expectant city.

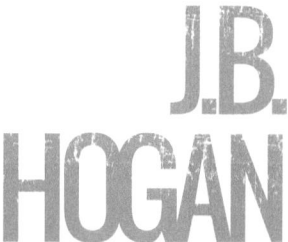

A Dry Country

Crossing the plains toward Amboseli
the earth was so dry
dust devils spun up into the air
like dirty brown tornadoes, moved
jerkily across the land, harming nothing
in their path.

The ground was barren, gray,
cracked and spread open
waiting, waiting for the rain,
rain that would not come.

Seven years and no rainy season,
rivers empty, trees unleafed,
animals nervous, chattery,
skin taught, ribs showing.

In the dying forests,
trees knocked down by elephants, upturned and
stripped of bark, roots—woods flattened

as if by bulldozer or heartless silent
airstrike from above.

By the shrinking waterholes,
deadly competition, prey and predator
intermixed in unexpected union, with
the weak and sick pushed aside;
and beyond: the dead, bellies bloated and
splitting open, decomposing,
lifeless eyes staring into the yellow heat
of the blinding, merciless sun.

Circling a Famous Author

He was sitting on a
black waiting room lounge chair
in Heathrow Airport and you could tell
he was a pretty tall man.

His hair was thick and tousled,
going gray at the edges, and
he wore big brown eye-glasses,
utilitarian rather than fashionable.

A guy across the room seemed to recognize him,
at first could only muster an occasional peek
over the edge of an overpriced paperback.

He might have been trying to come up with a
Billy Pilgrim reference or a pithy remark like
"everything is beautiful and nothing hurt" but
he didn't look like he could muster the courage.

Finally, he did make a move,
started walking around the waiting room
making loops around the famous author,
behind him, off to the right, then in front,
back to the left—repeat, repeat again.

By the second revolution it was all too obvious, but
the guy tried to be discreet, only daring a
furtive glance here and there,
hoping he was being way cool.

On loop three, the writer finally looked up,
took notice of the circler, shook his big head,
smiled a small, tired smile.

The guy hurried back to his seat and immediately
re-immersed himself in the neglected paperback.
Ten minutes passed before he dared
look over his book at the waiting room again.
By then the famous author was safely off to his plane and
the circler was safely formulating his own fiction
of the close encounter he had had with the
famous, unapproachable American writer.

Avenue of the Dead—Teotihuacan

They crossed the dusty Avenue of the Dead,
Pyramids of Sun and Moon on the left
in the distance towering above the dry Mexican land
walking into the less imposing Ciudadela with
its symmetrically aligned series of shorter
platforms on the way to see Quetzalcoatl,
feathered serpent god, with
newer structure covering old;
standing in between on a plywood plank
staring straight into the round eyes of water diety Tlaloc
amid the mystery of long forgotten
rituals and processions of
long forgotten Teotihuacanos,
priests and warriors replaced
by tourists, guides and trinket hawkers
under a blazing Meshican sun,
voices modulating loud or low
nearby and amid dozens of people
she said into a hot breeze:

"Can you hear it? Can you hear their sounds,
cries, pleas, people living and breathing, their past
gliding, floating on the winds of time?"
He listened carefully, for voices in the air,
felt wind on his face, listened more intently yet,
not wanting to disappoint:
"Yes," his uncertain answer, "I can. I can hear
them in the wind, across time."
She took his hand in hers and they started back
across the Ciudadela, returned to the Avenue of the Dead,
then down towards the great pyramids.
The bright sun shone down harshly,
but they blocked it out with raised hands,
walked on silently, certain in the fidelity
of time and wind.

Listen Up, America

Listen up, America, this is it, I've had it—up to here.

If I see, read or hear about one more zombie

I'm going to open your skull

and eat your black, rotting brain.

If I see, read or hear about one more vampire

I'm going to drive a wooden stake

through each and every one of your hearts.

If I have to listen to one more puffed up Idol

singing that god awful pablum pop

I'm going to pray for Dee Snyder to make a comeback.

If I have to listen to one more semi-literate hip-hopster

talking about and holding his junk

I'm going to pray for the return of Kurtis Blow,

Run DMC, and the Fat Boys.

If I have to listen to one more urban cowboy

singing about his tractor or his dog

I'm going to hogtie 'em all and play

Lefty Frizzell and Webb Pierce until the cows come home.

If I have to see one more televangelist

telling me about his personal relationship with god

I'm going to go downtown

and apply for admittance to atheists anonymous.

If I have to look at one more Kardashian skank

and be expected to pretend she's cool

I'm going to have to...

If I have to surf past one more episode of Survivor, the

Bachelorette or....

I'm going to...

If I have to watch one more TV newscaster

talking to me about news they don't understand

I'm going...

And if I have to listen to or read one more word

from some whining, complaining poet

then I'll just cut that poet off in mid-rant and stop....

Playa del Carmen

Days were slow and burning hot
shade-seeking, drinks by the beach
a trip to Tuluum with its cooling winds,
exploring the land.

Nights were calm and peaceful,
thought-seeking, restful in the banda,
listening to music floating in the air,
old, nostalgic, a sense of melancholy
for the many lost years.

Before the Hurricane

From Cancun, Mike Werth shared a taxi with a friendly, upscale American couple. The driver dropped them off just past the bus terminal in Playa del Carmen. With a quick goodbye, the couple hustled on to an expensive, close by resort while Mike looked for the Happy Turtle Hotel. With the aid of some helpful locals, he found it a few short blocks north of the bus station.

The Happy Turtle, unlike the more developed places closer to the town center, was actually a collection of little wood and plaster bandas, or mini-bungalows, just a short stroll from the beach. After checking in with the office, Mike tossed his stuffed backpack on the mosquito net-covered bed and went in search of Amy Perry.

Amy and Mike were friends from language school in Cuernavaca and she was a mutual friend of Mike's estranged girlfriend Jackie. Amy had agreed to meet Mike in the Yucatan when she completed a side trip to Cuba as part of a ten-day medical exchange program between the two hostile countries. They hooked up in Merida and bussed to Cancun where they spent a couple of days before she went ahead to meet some girlfriends in Playa del Carmen. Mike had the name of her hotel in Playa on a piece of paper and with his own cheaper lodgings taken care of went straight there.

Amy and her friends were at the Hotel Caribe next to the Blue Parrot Café, one of Playa's favorite on the beach watering holes. Mike couldn't locate the girls right away, so he sat down at one of the Parrot's umbrella-covered tables—an absolute necessity against the intensity of the Yucatan sun—and ordered a cold bottle of Superior.

While he sipped on the beer, Mike checked out the area around the Blue Parrot. On his left, just to the south, running up from the light brown, sandy beach, was a web of white string hammocks tied between large trees. It seemed to house a community of travelers who crashed for almost nothing right on the beach.

To his right, north of the Blue Parrot, was a long undeveloped stretch which he learned from a waiter was a topless beach—as, actually, was all the area around the Blue Parrot. That bit of information heightened Mike's appreciation for Playa and he celebrated with another Superior. He was about halfway through the second beer intently searching for signs of topless activity when Amy and her friends found him.

"Hey, Mike," Amy smiled. "You made it."

"I did," Mike stood to give her a hug. "Here I am."

He checked out the girls with Amy. One was shy and

dumpy, with long, stringy brown hair that looked like it could have used a good brushing sometime in the last few days. Her other friend was a bit too old to be referred to as a girl. She looked to be in her early 30s, was well-tanned and pretty. Mike assumed from her relaxed attitude and dark skin that she had probably been in the area for more than a few days. She also had a sort of perpetual smirk on her face and the way she cocked her head at Mike made him think she had sized him up quickly and was not terribly impressed.

"Mike," Amy introduced her friends, "this is Kerri. She's my good friend from the Bay Area. Kerri, Mike. Mike, Kerri."

"How are you?" Mike said. Kerri smiled shyly and looked down at the sand.

"I'm Paula," the tan friend did her own introduction. "Amy and I knew each other in Cuernavaca."

"Nice to meet you," Mike said. "Did we know each other there? That's where Amy and I met, too."

"I knew her before you came," Paula said cooly. Mike felt the chill of her exclusion.

"Oh."

"What ya drinking?" Amy asked, warming up the conversation.

"Superior," Mike said, "my favorite Mexican beer."

"I prefer Corona," Paula looked away from Mike towards the bar back up the beach.

"Well, I'll have a Superior, too," Amy said. "How about you Kerri?"

"I don't like beer," Kerri said. Paula snickered.

"Here comes a waiter," Mike announced as a small, Indian-looking man approached their table.

While the waiter took their drink orders, Mike tried not to stare at him. In profile, the young man looked exactly like the Mayan figures Mike had seen so often in relief on ancient ruins in the country. Of course, the Yucatan was Maya country but it was still impressive to see someone look so much like their progenitors. Mike said as much when the man left to get their drinks.

"I don't see it," Paula contradicted. "How can you generalize like that. Every person is different. He can hardly be one of the old Mayans."

"I'm not putting the guy down," Mike said, maybe a bit too defensively. "I think it's cool as hell. He looks like he could have walked right off one of the friezes from a ruin around here."

"He might find that kind of stereotyping offensive," Paula insisted.

"That is not what I was ..."

"H...here he comes back," Kerri stuttered.

"Check him out, Amy," Mike said, "see if I'm not right."

"Alright," Amy said. Paula rolled her eyes dramatically.

The waiter arrived with the drinks and while he was setting them on the table he and Mike carried on a simple, easy banter in Spanish. When the order had been dispersed, Mike gave the guy a decent tip in pesos.

"I kind of see what you mean, Mike," Amy said, she

and Mike tapped Superiors in a mini-toast. "He was very Mayan-looking."

"How cool is that?" Mike said, taking a deep draw on his beer. "Can you imagine looking so much like your relatives from two thousand years ago? Just amazing."

Paula didn't say anything else about the waiter but she assiduously avoided eye contact with Mike the rest of the time they were all together on the beach. That was pretty much okay with him.

—

Amy and Kerri shared one of the Hotel Caribe's one-room bungalows that faced the main building. Because they were separate structures from the big hotel itself and looked to have been built quite a bit earlier, Mike guessed the bungalows had been a different hotel in the past that had been swallowed up by the Caribe. He didn't know where Paula was staying but it was somewhere back up towards the center of town. With the sun dropping behind the beach palm trees, Mike gathered Amy and Kerri and they walked uptown to collect Paula.

"You have any special place up here you guys want to eat?" Mike asked as they neared an area with several eateries on both sides of the road.

"Any place is okay with me," Kerri said amiably.

"I think Paula had a little café she liked somewhere close by," Amy said.

"Sure," Mike replied, the image of a completely touristy, costly joint flashing through his mind.

"Hey, guys," Paula called out from a nearby doorway, shattering Mike's fantasy of self-righteously storming out of some overpriced Ugly American bar and grill.

But El Patio turned out to be the kind of local restaurant Mike always looked for himself. It was the kind of hybrid place where natives and travelers alike would eat. Not too expensive, with good portions, and at least some semblance, some feel of local ambience.

After dinner, while Kerri abstained, the others continued drinking beer and chatting. Eventually the conversation turned unavoidably to the status of Mike and Jackie's on again off again relationship. Amy was first to broach the subject.

"Has Jackie gotten in touch with you?" she asked.

"She said she might come out later this week," Mike replied, "but I haven't heard from her specifically."

"She hasn't called?" Mike shook his head.

"I thought she might call me when I was in Merida, before you came back."

"I'm sure she'll get in touch soon," Amy reassured him.

"I don't know."

"She'd be foolish not to come out and see you. You guys can work this out. I'm sure of it."

"Yeah, well."

On the way back from the restaurant, the group agreed to meet the next morning at a place about midway between Amy and Kerri's hotel and Mike's banda. Back at his place, alone, Mike indulged in a little self-pity and concocted a poem for Jackie based on a poem she wrote and left with him after they been to the ruins at Teotihuacan together.

Your Poem (As If), he scribbled a title down on a scratch sheet of paper. For a few moments he sat still, staring at the poem, then the words came to him:

I carried around your poem
as if it were currency in some market of souls,
as if having it would transform, create the past.
As if it could change me into something,
something I might not be.

I concealed it, hid it away,
away from those who would steal
what few hieroglyphs remain my own.

He paused, got a drink of water from a bottle he carried in his backpack and walked outside the banda to take in the night air. Somewhere in the distance heard music playing. A hit he remembered from the 1960s. He smiled into the darkness, let a wave of nostalgia pour over him, bathe him in old memories. Sighing, he went back inside and finished the poem.

I guarded it, hoarded it, watched it,
watched it as if something would happen.
I watched it; I watch it still.

And it's still there, between the pillowcase
with the other relics of my life.
Nothing has happened, yet,
it's just ink and paper---
it's still your poem.

It would work as a first draft anyway. He could work on it some more later. Carefully slipping the sheet of paper into one of the larger pockets of his backpack, he dug out a pair of swim trunks for the next morning and clicked off the light in the banda.

Next morning after breakfast he put on the swim trunks, grabbed a towel, and strolled out into the warm tropical morning to find Amy and her friends. He walked across the warming sand towards the beach and the agreed upon rendezvous point whistling softly and feeling unexpectedly happy. Passing between a couple of small buildings belonging to the Hotel Caribe, Mike suddenly halted under the shade of a palm tree.

"Uh," he involuntarily grunted.

Amy, Kerri and Paula were exactly where they had agreed to meet him. But to Mike's surprise, the three women were sitting under the palm tree topless. Breasts exposed to the warm breeze. Right there in front of him. He immediately tried to act like it was no big deal, something he saw every day. Mr. Cool.

"Hi, Mike," Amy smiled sweetly.

"H..h.hi," he stuttered, taking in her small, firm breasts, white from being covered by a bikini top.

"Hello," Kerri didn't look up.

"Good morning," Mike recovered some of his composure.

He noticed Kerri's large white breasts sagged a bit, something like her personality. He tried not to look at Paula but when she spoke he had no choice. There was no way to avoid seeing her perfect, tanned breasts. It figured. No wonder she oozed confidence. She looked great with no clothes on—the ultimate test.

"Did you get a good night's sleep?" Amy asked.

"Not bad."

"No call from Jackie?" Paula asked with a wry look at Mike.

"No," he looked away, "no call."

"Well," Amy said, "I'm sure she'll get in touch with you soon."

"Yeah," Mike grunted.

"Well, if we're through with last night," Paula said, "I don't know about you guys but I'd like to go to the beach pretty soon. How about it?"

"I want to do that," Kerri folded her arms over her breasts.

"I'm for it, too," Amy concurred.

"Why don't we meet up in about a half-hour or so?" Paula suggested.

"I'll meet you down there," Mike said, relieved to escape his bare-chested friends. "I'll be out by the Blue Parrot. Okay?"

"Sounds great," Amy said.

"Fine by me," Kerri agreed.

"See you then, big guy," Paula smiled wryly again.

"Sure," Mike said, turning quickly away from the women, "see you then."

—

While waiting for the women, Mike played on the beach. He splashed in shallow water and discovered a busty gringa frolicking topless in the gentle waves just north of the Blue Parrot. The powerful Yucatan sun reflected brightly off the water but Mike enjoyed the surf and the girl so much he didn't think about getting a sunburn. By the time the girls got to the beach, closer to an hour later rather than the suggested thirty minutes, Mike was already getting noticeably red.

"Ooh, Mike," Amy came up to him at the water's edge while Kerri and Paula put their things on a sun umbrella-covered table several yards off the beach. Mike was relieved to see that all three of them wore tops with their bathing suits. "You're looking a little lobsterish. You might want to be careful. Take a break out of the sun."

"Ah," Mike shook it off, "I'm having a great time out here splashing around."

"You know best, but you are getting more than pink."

"I'll be okay."

For the next couple of hours, they swam, body surfed and played in the ocean, coming on shore for the occasional cool and refreshing beer. But by noon, Mike knew Amy had been right. He was bright red. He felt the tightness of the burn, particularly in his legs. After lunch, he excused himself and went back to his banda. He felt unduly tired and decided to crash out for a while.

When he awoke, it was nearly dusk and he was burning up. Everywhere. His face, body, especially the legs. And he had a high fever. It was a really bad sunburn. When the girls came by to invite him to go eat he begged off. Amy wanted to stay and make sure he was okay but he thanked her and told her to go on. During the night, the sunburn got worse and worse. He drifted in and out of a feverish sleep, the pain not allowing him to rest properly.

In the morning he was blistered up and when the girls came by to see if he wanted to join them on an excursion to the ruins at Tuluum he again declined. Amy was even harder to dissuade from watching out for him this time but with Paula's practical help he was able to convince her to go and enjoy the trip.

All day he lay in bed feeling poorly and drifting in and out of a fitful sleep. Late in the afternoon, Amy came by after the trip to Tuluum and brought Mike a bottle of water and some orange juice. She again offered to stay and care for him but he assured her he would be alright.

"Are you hungry?" she asked. "I'll be glad to go get you something."

"No, I'm not hungry at all. The water and juice will really help. And I have some snacks in my backpack if I really get hungry."

"I'm sorry you got so burned."

"It wasn't your fault. I'm the idiot who didn't realize how hot this Yucatan sun is."

"It's really strong."

"Was Tuluum great?" Mike tried to change the subject.

"Wonderful. It was airy and with a beautiful view of the ocean. Just terrific."

"That's good," Mike said, his eyes closing involuntarily.

"I better go and let you rest."

"Thanks for checking on me."

"Kerri and I have to catch our flight out of Cancun in the morning and Paula is going to visit friends up at Isla de Mujeres," Amy said. "I hate to say goodbye like this."

"It's okay," Mike said, "I appreciate you coming by."

"Maybe we'll run into each other in Mexico City or Cuernavaca again."

"Sure. Maybe."

"Maybe with Jackie even."

"May be."

After Amy left, Mike lay in the dark of the banda thinking about Jackie, imagining she still might call or leave a message. Lightheaded from fever and uncomfortable from the sunburn pain, he drifted in and out of consciousness listening to music wafting in from somewhere down by the beach. Someone played an old Doors album. It made Mike think of the 60s, the feeling of freedom and hopefulness he had then, and he imagined the music came from the neo-hippies camped out in the hammocks by the beach.

As he drifted off to sleep he allowed the nostalgia of the past overwhelm him, take the sting out of his sunburned and presently unhappy situation. Playa del Carmen felt like it was in some sort of time warp, where the feeling of that earlier decade still existed, was still vibrant and alive. He smiled to think so and as he fell asleep his last thought was how glad he was to have known Jackie even if he would never see her again. Everything was going to be alright.

It took Mike two more full days before the sunburn let up enough to allow him to travel. On the third morning after the girls left, he took a bus into Cancun and bought a ticket for Mexico City. He still had friends in Cuernavaca and would go see them, start anew. He would find someone else, either here in Mexico or back home. He knew there was someone else out there for him, he was sure of it.

Later that fall, just weeks after he had returned alone to the states, Mike read that Hurricane Hugo ripped through Playa del Carmen destroying all the older places like the Happy Turtle. In the ruins of the hurricane, Playa had rebuilt itself in a more modern image. Everything was fancy now, expensive and big. Large exclusive resorts replaced the quaint little hotels and such that were the last remains of an earlier age.

It saddened him to hear of the change but he had his memories. He had been there when things were still different, when there were still reminders of a simpler world. The old way might be gone now but he remembered how things had once been and that, poignant as it might seem, was all one could expect. It was sure better than having no memories of the old way at all. Much better than that.

Man of Straw

The 1% you worship, their fairy tales you trust;
you've fallen on the sword, eaten their swill,
drunk the Kool-Aid, swallowed the line—which
you now regurgitate at will.

Your obscurant ramblings expose
a regrettable paucity of wit,
the humor in your lines is weak—
even for a lonely git.

You're a double-dipping snake thief
with insides made of hay,
you pen pathetic gibberings
but have nothing real to say.

Yet it's verbal swordplay you seem to seek
looking to enjoin and push the battle,
but you'll need a better weapon,
a sharper one, one of stronger mettle.

For like the silent flapping of a butterfly
impaled upon an eagle's claw,
your feeble arguments are soft and hollow,
befitting a useless man of straw.

Pack Runner

I.

Pack runner, ankle-grabber of the old,
the weak, the lame,
killer of youth.

Small, gray with
killer's teeth and breath,
scavenging for a meal.

It seems so unfair—
the gnawing hunger with
so much nearby;
fearful jerky movements
circling the other scavengers.

There's one, then two, a half dozen, twenty or more,
more than the little pack can
chase away, away from the kill,
taking all of it, all, nothing left.

Nothing left for the defeated pack but
move away, run away, together,
searching for old ankles to grab or the
weak, lame, something stray,
young—to corner and kill.

II.

Packed, banded, snarling,
circling the isolated one,
wolf-like, teeth bared, gums exposed,
flesh-streaked, bloody dangling.

The one cut out fights back,
swelling up, ready to run,
full of fear, hurt, fight,
near helpless but
not lost yet.

Then moving off, successful, loud braying,
not satisfied, still hungry, predator without grace,
yapping, high-pitched whine, victorious
without bravery or fill.

Dad

My mother's father came to live with us
when I was just a kid.
We called him Dad even though
he was really our grandpa.
He was tall and thin with mostly white hair and
old shoulders, tired and bent.

He turned seventy-five when I was just four
and sat most times in a big worn chair,
holding burning cigarettes in long yellowed fingers.
He treated me special, like a little beggar king and
I wore his hat for playing cowboy—
he spoiled me every day.

When I was six and went off to school,
scared and insecure, he was there
at home waiting for me to come back,
letting me clump around the house in his old
cowboy boots.

When I was seven he began to fade;
his old body wearing out.
Then early one winter morning
he took his own life.

After, some people said that it was a sin,
that only god can give or take life;
but I knew Dad was a good man
and no god worth the name
would ever judge him
for ending his mortal pain.

A Loud Hum

Through a nearby window the hum of insects floated in on a wave of hot sticky air. A grasshopper hit the screen with a muted metallic sound. A chicken or some small animal rustled in the dry grass beside the house.

He got up from the bed and walked through the living room for a drink. The water was cool but tasteless. He set the glass down and went back into the living room. One of the dogs on the front porch barked listlessly. Out on the main road he heard the dusty whine of wheels on dirt. He listened until he was sure the car had passed, then walked to the screen door and looked out.

A dog started to get up but lay right back down in the shade. To the left of the house, a rooster poked his head around the side of a decaying out building at the edge of the overgrown front yard. There was the loud hum of insects again.

He stood by the door for a few minutes, then went over and sat on the arm of the couch. He shook his head back and forth as if trying to clear it of something. Picking up a copy of the post newspaper, he thumbed through it without interest. In a moment, he tossed the paper down, rose, sat down, then stood up again and went into the bedroom.

For a quarter of an hour he lay on his back in his khaki pants and t-shirt staring at the ceiling, listening to the outside sounds, waiting. He was sure he'd forgotten something but didn't know what. So he waited. But it didn't come. He waited. It wasn't coming.

Before he realized he had dozed off, he woke up. He hadn't slept long and he knew he'd dreamed. He thought of the wall closet and got up to get the box from the top shelf. His dog tags jingled against his chest. It was still early and he wasn't sure yet. But he had to get the box. It was still early.

It was beginning to get late when he went out for a walk. He walked down the path behind the house and tried not to think. On his left he passed the cabin that had once been a work shop. It was old and rundown now. Weeds grew out of its foundation and most of the windows were broken. He passed it by.

He walked to a small creek below the house, feeling the ground's hardness through the worn-thin soles of his brogans. He crossed the stream, pausing midway to balance on a flat, white rock and watch minnows and crawdads swim in the clear water. The creek reminded him of some other place, some other time. It seemed like a very long time ago. Looking at the water made him thirsty but he did not get a drink. The sun was blocked off by the trees here and he lingered a while to enjoy the cool air.

Down the path he passed an ice cold spring, but again didn't drink. Just beyond the spring, in a warm clearing, he found the decaying stump of a once huge oak and sat down on it. Across the clearing he could see a group of blue jays harassing a summer-thin squirrel. They squawked and dove, driving the small squirrel into the nearby bush and then up into another tree well away from their nests. For a moment he felt sorry for the squirrel.

When the sun dipped below the tallest tree beyond the clearing, he headed back home. In the backyard he stepped over some old cans and bottles. They reminded him of when he was a boy. He smiled briefly. Climbing the steps slowly, he quietly entered through the back door. The house was still and the kitchen was cool. He reached for the ice-box door and pulled it part way open. He let it close on its own. It did not shut completely, but it didn't seem to matter.

In the bedroom, the box lay haphazardly where he'd left it. Sitting on the edge of the bed, he pulled the box to him and, taking a deep breath, opened it. Outside it was so quiet, it seemed the whole world had gone mute. He shook his head. That still didn't help. He focused his attention on the open box. He reached inside it and felt the cool metal with his fingertips. The metal was blue and smooth and personal. Several moments passed. He kept his hand against the metal.

The sun was near the western horizon and the heat-tranquilized animals were just beginning to stir when the sharp, cracking sound came from the house. The chickens fluttered about and scooted into the tall grass. The dogs howled and barked. When the echoing sound had passed, they quieted down, but cast nervous glances at the house.

It was about ten in the morning when the olive drab car turned off the main road into the long narrow lane leading to the house. Several men in olive drab uniforms got out of the car, passed the curious dogs, and moved cautiously towards the house. The dogs rose and followed to sniff around the men, but the chickens just clucked comfortably as they pecked away undisturbed at the yard. Flies buzzed loudly in the warm air. The day was calm and beautiful. There was no sound from the house.

poetry

Down Highway 65

South of Sedalia, road
winding through farm country
cold, dull winter gray,
little town sped past
not stopping now nor ever
just passing by fallen, decaying
houses, crumbled-in shells of
buildings, stone blocks collapsed
on foundation, forgotten,
ignored, lost memory
faded in winter day
growing dim with the light,
short day of winter
never to become spring.

J.B.
HOGAN

Grocery List

Go out, she said, and get us something for supper.

He went, but he didn't want to.
Bread, eggs, milk, cheese.
All the staples, the essence,
the basis of life.

But what life, a life without spice,
without cinnamon, not even ginger,
what kind of life would that be.

Apple juice, he remembered, that, too,
some kind of Krusteaz mix, for a cake, a cobbler,
maybe a bread, sweet and spiced—the cinnamon
or ginger – covered with melting butter and
then a cold glass of milk finishing off dessert.

It would be alright, then, when he got home,
they would be happy again, she would bake him

a special cake or bread and they would be full again, full of bread or cake and the feelings they once had for one another, before cake or bread was necessary for them to be happy.

He Is Coming

He is coming, you know,
you can feel his presence growing,
every day, every night.

There's a tightening up with a
loosening up—rest is
hard to come by, sleep
disrupted, disturbed, dreams
strange and chilling.

Yes, he's coming, and you're the
desperado at the station waiting,
waiting for that dark train,
the black locomotive to nowhere.

He Liked It That Much

El Machete was a little *jíbaro,* the Caribbean equivalent of a hillbilly, from the central highlands. He'd been convicted of hacking his wife to pieces with the same sharp machete he used for working in the cane fields. Somehow he escaped La Piedra, the maximum security prison on Boca Tierra, and disappeared into the crowded streets of San Sebastian. For a *jíbaro,* he showed remarkable skill at eluding the sophisticated tracking techniques of the Boca Tierran and San Sebastian police.

Once he fled out the back of a rundown shack in the projects as the cops were coming in the front. Another time he'd been chased down the blue brick streets of Old San Sebastian only to vanish just when the police thought they had him trapped.

The escape that captured the imagination of the entire island, however, had *El Machete* eluding the law on a fat-tired, run down bicycle. The cops raced up and down alleys and side streets in their VW squad cars, sirens blaring, red lights flashing, but *El Machete* somehow got away again. The police were red-faced, the media had the hottest story in years, and the nation got what most nations revel in, even crave, an outlaw the system can't catch, control, or conquer.

"Get this cabrón," the governor told the national police. "I don't care how."

"I want this son of a bitch in custody," the mayor demanded of his police chief, "immediately. If not sooner."

The police fanned out all over San Sebastian. They hauled in prostitutes from the tourist section, rounded up informants, stopped people on the street, chased cars around town with weapons dangling wildly out the windows of unmarked vehicles, made a timely push on leftists and subversives.

Early one morning, a couple of weeks after the famous bicycle escape, the police raided a house near Boca Tierra's main university said to be occupied by a group of socialist students. The students were presumed to be harboring *El Machete*, darling populist hero of the press. The leftists were sure to help anybody like that, the police reasoned, even if he was a brutal murderer.

The students were sleeping when the raid began. One couple slept in the master bedroom, two men and a girl slept in three twin beds in the other bedroom. In the living room, one young man slept on the couch while another lay on the floor wrapped in a sheet.

"What the...?" The youth in the master bedroom cried out as the window shattered and several men clambered into the room. He could hear the sounds of the rest of the raid as other windows and the heavy front door were broken into. The girl leapt up beside him, exposing her slim, brown body, naked except for a pair of flimsy panties. The police made a concerted effort to keep her out of bed and standing, arms across her breasts, in the middle of the room.

In a matter of moments, the entire group was collected in the living room, with the exception of the young man sleeping on the floor. In trying to flee, he had been caught at the door and was still there, lying face down, a .38 revolver held to his head by a blue-uniformed officer. The naked girl tried to cover herself as best she could but one of the police, an older pot-bellied man, slapped her arms away from her chest. Several minutes went by before the chief detective entered the house. A police sergeant followed closely behind.

"Very good roundup, Sergeant Rivera," the detective said. "Now where is he?"

"Uh, who, Lieutenant?" the sergeant asked.

"Rivera," the lieutenant barked.

"Yes, sir," Sergeant Rivera said quickly, "I'll determine that right now. Robles! Angel Robles!" The pot-bellied cop hurried from beside the naked girl.

"Sir," he said to the sergeant.

"Where is he, Robles?" Rivera demanded. "Where's *El Machete?* You're the one who called in the raid, weren't you?"

"He must be here, sir," Robles pointed to the students.

"*Idiota,*" Rivera bawled, "I suppose he found the fountain of youth, did he?"

"Sir?" Robles scratched his head.

"These are children, Robles, children. *El Machete* is an old man. What were you thinking? Lieutenant Marín is waiting. Waiting for us to produce the killer. Is he here Robles?"

Before Robles could answer, another uniformed policeman rushed into the house and ran up to Lt. Marín who immediately headed for the door.

"Come on Rivera," he yelled. *"El Machete* was cornered but escaped again. Vehicles are in pursuit. He's halfway across town. Come on. Let these people go. Now!"

"Yes, sir," Rivera signaled the other officers to release the students and join the chase for *El Machete*. "Let them go." Angel started to leave too, but Rivera stopped him.

"Stay out of this Robles," Rivera snarled, "keep away." He pushed Robles out of the way and then called to an officer standing at the back of all the activity. "Muñoz... front and center."

"Yes, sir," Muñoz came to attention before Sgt. Rivera.

"Get your partner out of here," Rivera ordered, "and keep him under control. You got that?"

"Yes, sir," Muñoz addressed Rivera's back as the sergeant whirled and stormed out of the house.

Muñoz and Robles were left with the students. The students, relieved but becoming indignant, talked among themselves. One of them made an obscene gesture at Robles.

"Let's get the hell out of here," Muñoz said, pushing his partner toward the door. "In a few minutes these students will be ready to kill us... and I can't say I blame them."

"I'm hungry, Hector," Robles said, "let's go eat breakfast somewhere."

"*Ave María*," Muñoz shook his head, "Blessed Virgin."

—

Officers Muñoz and Robles breakfasted semi-American style at the Nuevo Pio-Pio on warm, buttered *pan de agua* and *cafe con leche*. As the officers savored their bread and coffee, an old *campesino* across from them shoveled down a meal of chicharrones and *mofongo con caldo*. The heavy mixture of fried chicken strips and blob of fried green bananas drowned in a broth made Robles grimace as he watched the man eat.

"That *jíbaro* eats like an animal," he told Muñoz, "he makes me sick."

"Don't look at him," Muñoz said.

"Disgusting."

"He's just an old man. They finished their bread and coffee.

"We better get back on patrol," Robles said, "Sergeant Rivera's a little angry."

"A little," Muñoz laughed, "he's ready to bust you down to traffic control."

"Hmph," Robles grunted.

The officers walked to the cashier and paid. They passed by the *jíbaro* on their way out.

"I ought to arrest him for eating like a pig," Robles muttered.

The old man looked up at the policemen and smiled. He was missing most of his front teeth and *caldo* ran down from his mouth onto his unshaven chin. Robles belched and looked away. Muñoz snickered. The *jíbaro* kept smiling.

"Díos mío!" Robles exclaimed, as the officers went out the door. "My God!"

Back at the table, the legendary fugitive known to all Boca Tierrans, except himself, as *El Machete,* continued wolfing down his bowl of food. He really liked the big city of San Sebastian. The people were friendly and you could always get lots of food, and pretty cheap. Good tasting food, too. He might just stay in San Sebastian a good long time, he told himself, drinking the rest of the *mofongo con caldo* from the bowl. It might be a nice place to live. He liked it that much.

From 32,000 feet

they looked like a
large field of white crosses
arranged in an asymmetric rectangle—
white crosses from some mass crucifixion, a
Golgotha or Appian Way many times over, but
they were just wind turbines
dotting the Texas countryside,
generating electricity for Dallas
maybe or Fort Worth, just an
energy field, and not a metaphor,
religious or otherwise.

Somebody's Father

That was somebody's father
lying up there in the open casket
at the front of the room.

Somebody's father—still, silent,
slack-jawed in death,
still, forever.

The crowd was still, too, while the preacher preached
that the old man was in a better place now
that he was somewhere where somebody's savior was.

Maybe the preacher didn't know the old man very well.
Maybe he thought it was somebody else that died.
Maybe this wasn't the right room for the service.

Because this man hadn't been
any of those things the preacher said;
he wasn't like that at all.

He was just somebody's father
lying there still, silent;
just somebody's father,
lying up there in the open casket
at the front of the room—
still, silent, forever.

Kingfisher and the Caraway Seed

When the kingfisher flew
up from the south
it caused quite a stir among the
crowds that flocked to see the
legendary bird, the bird
that came north to plant the
caraway seed among a packed
group of contending rows
none of which were the right soil
from which their own seeds
could possibly grow.

But over the next eight days the
kingfisher darted here and there
with its little seed, tempting this
field, teasing that, until the
ground had been saturated with
hope and promise.

Its mission done, the kingfisher
flew home, back south, while the
fast-growing seed took root,
matured, blossomed, became
the star of the field—a new kind,
a first kind, a real winner.

Back down south, among the
bayous and the bald-cypress trees, the
kingfisher—full of hubris from its
northern victory, flew too close to the
swampy, swollen land, too close to those
who hated its success, those who would
dare to shoot such a rare bird and
bring it crashing, empty of
pride, joy or hope,
to the Louisiana ground.

The Rubicon

Once passed—its clear water
muddied from countless tramplings,
the far shore easily breached,
destiny's hand already played,
the future closer, the past dropped away—
is the outcome unalterable,
frozen in place for all time to come?
Is there no turning back
no change allowed;
must the rigid journey
play out its one, its fixed course?
Even at capitol's edge, then,
is there no way out,
no command left to halt the march?
Too late then, it must be,
for republic, for hope,
too late to withdraw,
to turn away, turn around,
head back, back across the restraining stream
to wait on the near shore for the shallow river

to flow clean and pure once more,
to retreat then from water's edge;
and go back, back onto dry land,
back to when it was nothing but a narrow, shallow stream,
before arrogance and imperial ambition
made crossing its rocky waters
a matter of political necessity, and
unbridled, destructive pride.

J. B. Hogan is a prolific and award-winning author. He grew up in Fayetteville, Arkansas, but moved to Southern California in 1961 before entering the U. S. Air Force in 1964. After the military, he went back to college, receiving a Ph.D. in English from Arizona State University in 1979.

J. B. has published over 250 stories and poems. His novels, *The Apostate*, *Living Behind Time* and *Losing Cotton*—as well as his local baseball history book, *Angels in the Ozarks*—are available on Amazon.com.

J. B. currently serves as Past President of the Washington County (AR) Historical Society. He plays upright bass in East of Zion, a family band that specializes in bluegrass-flavored Americana music.

Facebook: J.B. Hogan
www.thejbhogan.com